Praise for
RODMAN PHILBRICK'S
The Last Book in the Universe

"Enriched by allusions to nearly lost literature and full of intriguing, invented slang, the skillful writing paints two pictures of what the world could look like in the future — the burned-out Urb and the pristine Eden — then shows the limits and strengths of each. Philbrick, author of *Freak the Mighty* (1993), has again created a compelling set of characters that engage the reader with their courage and kindness in a painful world that offers hope, if no happy endings."

—*Kirkus Reviews*

"There is much to admire in Philbrick's tale of a postapocalyptic future. There's stubborn hope and strength of conviction in the book's moving conclusion, and Philbrick has created some memorable characters in this fast-paced adventure, which will leave readers musing over humanity's future."   —*Booklist*

"Enthralling, thought-provoking, and unsettling, Philbrick's newest novel hurls readers into the Urb, a bleak future world of gray skies, acid rain, savage behavior, and endless cement. Philbrick's creation of a futuristic dialect, combined with striking descriptions of a postmodern civilization, will convincingly transport readers to Spaz's world."

—*Publishers Weekly*

"Add this to your library shelves, display it with your quick-pick titles, and share it in your classrooms. Philbrick has outdone himself; this futuristic novel will stimulate thought and discussion among contemporary readers."   —*VOYA*

RODMAN PHILBRICK

The Last Book in the Universe

Scholastic Inc.

New York Toronto London Auckland Sydney
Mexico City New Delhi Hong Kong Buenos Aires

No part of this publication may be reproduced, stored in a retrieval system, or transmitted in any form or by any means, electronic, mechanical, photocopying, recording, or otherwise, without written permission of the publisher. For information regarding permission, write to Scholastic Inc., Attention: Permissions Department, 557 Broadway, New York, NY 10012.

This book was originally published in hardcover by the Blue Sky Press in 2000.

ISBN 0-439-08759-7

27 26 25 24 23 22 21 20 19 18 17 16   5 6 7 8 9/0

Printed in the U.S.A.   40

Designed by Kathleen Westray

FOR LYNN HARNETT, ALWAYS,

AND FOR EVERYONE

WHO KEEPS ON READING

CHAPTER ONE

They Call Me
Spaz

IF YOU'RE READING this, it must be a thousand years from now. Because nobody around here reads anymore. Why bother, when you can just probe it? Put all the images and excitement right inside your brain and let it rip. There are all kinds of mind-probes — trendies, shooters, sexbos, whatever you want to experience. Shooters are violent, and trendies are about living in Eden, and sexbos, well you can guess what sexbos are about. They say probing is better than anything. I wouldn't know because I've got this serious medical condition that means I'm allergic to electrode needles. Stick one of those in my brain and it'll kick off a really bad seizure and then — total mind melt, lights out, that's all, folks.

They call me Spaz, which is kind of a mope name, but I don't mind, not anymore. I'm talking into an old voicewriter program that prints out my words because I was there when the Bully Bangers went to wheel the Ryter for his sins, and I saw what they saw, and I heard what they heard, and it kind of turned my brain around.

The Bangers have the latch on my part of the Urb, which means they control everybody and everything between Eastie and the Pipe. A million people, maybe more. Nobody really knows how many, because nobody can count that high. Why bother? All you gotta know is, if you live here you're either down with the Bangers or you might as well be dead. There's no escape because every part of the Urb is latched by one gang or another. The only escape is Eden, and you can't get in there unless you're a proov, and if you're genetically improved you'd never leave in the first place, so forget about Eden.

I used to belong to a family unit, with a foster mom and dad and my little sister, Bean, but that's over, and I don't want to talk about what happened, or how unfair it was. Not yet. The less said about that the better, because if there's one thing I learned from Ryter it's that you can't always be looking backward or something will hit you from the front.

Ryter was this gummy that changed my life, and if you're reading this, maybe he changed the world, too. Gummies are what we call old people, and the Ryter was so ancient, the hair on his chin beard was as white as bone, and most of his teeth were gone. Even his skin was old and worn out and so thin, it looked like if you held him up to the light you'd see right through him.

The way I got to know Ryter is this: The Bangers sent me to bust him down. As far as I was concerned at the time, he was just another gummy scheduled for cancellation, so why not rip him off?

And that's exactly what I did.

CHAPTER TWO

Stealing Is
My Job

THE STACKBOX WHERE Ryter lives is out at the Edge, alongside of the Pipe. The Pipe is broken now, but in the backtimes they say it carried billions of gallons of water into the Urb. Fresh, clean water that didn't have to be boiled and filtered before you drank it. Water so pure, you could swim in it without shriveling. I figure that's a made-up story, like a lot of the backtimer talk. In case you don't know, the backtimes were before the Big Shake, when everything supposedly was perfect, and everybody lived rich.

Personally, I doubt the backtimes ever existed. It's like a story you tell to make yourself feel better, that's all. The kind of story that starts with my real mom is a rich proov and my real dad is a latchboss and someday they'll rescue me and we'll all move to Eden and live happily ever after. Yeah, right. That only happens in the trendies. In real life nobody comes to your rescue.

Believe me, I know.

Anyhow, the stacks. Nobody owns the stacks, and if you squat in one long enough, I guess you can call it home — if home is a little concrete box stacked ten high, in rows of a hundred. They say in the back-times they used the boxes to store all the things they owned, but the only things stored there now are losers. Assorted mopes and needlebrains, and gummies like the Ryter.

You can smell the stacks before you see 'em, on account of there's no plumbing and the 'boxers have to use the ground like animals. The strange thing is, at first glance it looks like nobody lives there. Nearby is this old industrial warehouse that sort of caved in long ago, and the rusty beams and rubble are strewn around, which makes it hard to walk without tripping over stuff. I can hear the scratchy noise of rats scurrying out of my way, and when there's rats, the humans are sure to be close, but where are they?

Hiding, it turns out. As I get closer, a small, smeary face peeks up from behind a pile of rubble, and then there's a whistle, a warning signal, and the noise of people scrambling to hide themselves, like they're afraid of something. Me, probably. They assume I'm one of the Bully Bangers, come to bust them down or worse, which is pretty close to the truth, even if I don't like to admit it. I'm not officially down with the Bangers, but the gang boss, Billy Bizmo, he sort of likes me for some reason. When he heard I lost my family unit he said make room for the spaz boy, and they did.

So the deal is, I'm here to steal. Stealing is my job. It's how I stay alive. Either you pay tribute to the Bangers, which means they get half of everything that sticks to your hands, or the Bangers decide you're no longer among the living. Which makes things very simple, even if sometimes you feel sort of bad about ripping off people who are even poorer than you are.

Steal or die. That's what it all comes down to. "Be a Banger or Be Gone," as the saying goes.

Anyhow, this little face pokes up again from the rubble and looks at me with big, scared eyes and I go, "Hey! Don't move!" and he freezes.

The little face belongs to a little kid, maybe five years old, although he's got at least a million years' worth of dirt on his cheeks. I bend down to look at him closer and a tear cuts through the dirt, which makes me feel bad, even though I haven't hurt the little guy, or ripped him off or anything. Not yet.

"Hey," I go. "Can you talk?"

Little Face nods. Now there are two tears melting the dirt on his cheeks.

Keeping my voice real low and gentle, I go, "You want a choxbar? All you got to do, show me the way to Ryter's stackbox. You know where he lives?"

I take the choxbar from my pocket and unwrap it so he can see, but he looks even more scared. I break off half and give it to him and go, "Eat it. Come on, it ain't going to kill you," and he kind of flinches and that's when I realize he's never had a choxbar and he thinks it might be poison. I break off another little piece and put it in my mouth and go, "Mmmmmm, good," and finally he eats a piece and waits for it to explode. When the taste starts to hit him, all velvety chocolate, Little Face finally stops crying. "Told you it was good," I say. "Now what about the geez they call Ryter? Where can I find him, huh?"

Little Face walks me through the rows of stack-boxes. He doesn't say anything; he's too busy sucking the taste out of the choxbar, or maybe he's still too scared to talk. Whatever, when he gets to a certain row he stops and just stands there.

I go, "Is this it?"

Instead of saying yes, he runs away.

One of the boxes on the lower row is open. Usually you have to bust down the door, which is why they call it a "bustdown," of course, but this place is wide open. Like the mope who lives there is saying, Go ahead, rip me off. Which makes me think he could be waiting inside to cut my red and splash me.

That's how you have to think — real cautious and paranoid — when you're on a bustdown. Mostly the mopes don't dare fight back, because of what the gang would do to them, but sometimes you get a suicidal mope, and then all bets are off.

As it turns out, the mope *is* waiting inside, but he doesn't try to fight. He's this gummy with white, white hair and shiny eyes — that's the first thing I notice, how his eyes kind of light up from deep inside his head. He's wearing a loose, ragged tunic that's stitched together, made from even older rags, which means he's even poorer than most of the curb people.

"Hello, young man," he goes. "Welcome to my humble abode."

He's sitting behind this crummy old crate he uses as a desk, resting his chin on his hands and looking at me with those shiny old eyes. Real casual, like he couldn't care less about getting ripped off.

"Humble abode" must be backtimer talk for "stack-box" or "crudhole" or whatever, but I'm not there to flapjaw with some gummy old mope. I just want to get in, take whatever junk he's hoarding, and get out.

That's when I notice that all his stuff is lined up by the door, ready to go.

"I've been expecting you," he explains. "Word gets around out here in the stacks. You are, I assume, an emissary from the Bully Bangers?"

I nod.

"Come on in," he says. "Make yourself at home."

I go, "Huh?" like, What are you, twisted? You *want* a bustdown? You *want* to get ripped? Are you brainsick or what? Except all I really say is, "Huh?" because the rest is implied, which is a word I later got from Ryter.

"I heard about the Bully Bangers giving me up," he says, like it's no big deal. "Bound to happen, sooner or later. Help yourself, son. Everything of value is over there by the door."

He points out a tote bag with a few cruddy items inside. An old alarm-clock vidscreen; a streetball mitt so old it's made of molded plastic; a mini-stove with the power cord all neat and coiled. It doesn't amount to much, but there's enough for a few credits at the pawn mart. Better than usual for the stacks.

"Go on," he says, urging me on. "Take it."

Normally I would, but there's something not normal about the whole situation. Like the way he coiled up the cord to the mini-stove. You know you're going to get ripped and you do that? Is it some kind of trick or what?

It's like he knows what I'm thinking, because the next thing he says is, "This isn't my first bustdown. Just thought I'd make it easier for us both. Go on, take it. Take it all."

"Yeah? What else you got?" I ask, closing in on the old geez. Because he must be hiding something. Everybody tries to hide something.

He smiles at me, which makes his wrinkled old face sort of glow, in a weird way. Like he wants an excuse to smile, no matter what happens. "What makes you think I've got anything else?" he asks.

That's when I see there's a pile of something under the crate, and he's been sitting there in front of it, hoping I wouldn't notice. "What's this?" I go.

"Nothing of value," he says, pretending to yawn. "Just a book, is all."

And that's when I know he's lying.

CHAPTER THREE

Those Who Remember

I GO, "LIAR! Books are in libraries. Or they used to be."

The man called Ryter starts to say something and then he stops, like I've given him something important to think about. "Interesting," he says. "You're aware that the things called 'books' used to be stored in libraries. That was long before you were born, so how did you know?"

I shrug and say, "I heard, is all. When I was a little kid. About how things used to be before the Shake."

"And you remember everything you hear?"

"Pretty much," I say. "Doesn't everybody?"

The old gummy chuckles. "Not hardly. Most of 'em, they've had their brains softened by needle probes and they can't really retain much. Long-term memory is a thing of the past, no pun intended. The only ones left who can remember books are a few old geezers like me. And, apparently, you."

Now that I think about it, I know what he's talking about. I've always had a lot of old stuff in my head that everybody else seems to have forgotten.

"What else do you remember?" Ryter asks.

"What do you care?"

The gummy gives me a look, like he wants to memorize me or something. "Remembering things is very important to a writer. Before you can put it down on paper, you have to remember what happened."

"Put what down on paper? What are you spewing, huh?"

He takes a piece of paper from the pile of stuff he's trying to hide in the crate. The paper is covered with small black marks. I hold it up close to my eyes, to see if there's anything hidden there, inside the paper, but to me the marks look like the footprints of bugs.

"I used to use a voicewriter like everybody else, but it got ripped off," Ryter explains. "So I went back to basics. I write down each word by hand, like they did in the backtimes. Primitive, but it works."

I go, "But what's the point? What are you putting inside your 'book'?"

Ryter looks at me for a while before he says, "Sorry, son, but that's between me and myself. I can tell you this much: My book is the work of a lifetime."

"You're wasting your time," I tell him. "Nobody reads books anymore."

Ryter nods sadly. "I know. But someday that may change. And if and when it does, they'll want stories — experiences — that don't come out of a mindprobe needle. People will want to read books again, someday."

" 'They'?" I go. "Who do you mean?"

"Those who will be alive at some future date," he says.

Those who will be alive at some future date. I don't know why, but the way he says it gives me a shiver. Because I'd never thought about the future. You want to be down with the Bangers, you can't think about the future. There's only room for the right here, and the want-it-now. The future is like the moon. You never expect to go there, or think about what it might be like. What's the point if you can't touch it or steal it or shoot it into your brain?

"What's your story, son?" Ryter asks, like he really wants to know.

I go, "I don't have a story."

Almost before I get the words out, he's shaking his head, like he knew what I was going to say and can't wait to disagree. "Everybody has a story," he insists.

"There are things about your life that are specific only to you. Secret things you know."

When he says "secret things," a chill goes up from the base of my spine to the top of my head and makes my brain feel numb and frosty. Because there's certain things I can't stand to remember and the last thing I want to do is share them with some old gummy.

"You're zoomed," I tell him. "Crazy as a cockroach. And I'm out of here."

Before I go he makes me take his stuff. The ministove, the alarm-clock vidscreen, all his junk.

"You'll need this," he says. "I know how it works with the gangs."

So I take his crummy stuff. I rip the old geez off. I feel weird and sort of sick about it, but it doesn't matter, because I'll never see him again. And if you can't see something, it doesn't really exist, right?

Right?

CHAPTER FOUR

The Girl with
Sky-Colored Eyes

ON THE WAY BACK to my cube I get sighted by a proov, which scares me halfway dead.

I'm cutting through this old falling-down place they call the Maximall, which used to be full of trade stalls in the backtimes. They say every stall was piled high with jewelry and fancy clothes and mysterious gizmos and lots of shiny things nobody really remembers anymore. They say there were stalls with ten thousand different kinds of choxbars instead of just the one. Probably that's a lie about the choxbars, but I'd like to believe it. There are still a few traders at the Maxi, but they're protected by bristlebars and cutwire, and the teks will beat you with stunstiks if you haven't got anything worth trading.

I'm keeping my distance when a takvee pulls up to one of the stalls. "Takvee" is slang for Tactical Urban Vehicle, the heavily armored, cyber-driven vans that proovs use to get around the Urb. If you're paying attention, you already know a proov is a genetically improved human being. They're the people who own the world, or at least the part of it they call Eden.

You can always tell a proov because they're all tall and beautiful and healthy-looking. The other way to tell a proov is how they look at you if you're a normal. A proov can't help shuddering inside when he sees a normal. We give them the creeps. We're a reminder of what human beings are like when they're not born perfect, and I guess if you're a proov, the very idea of imperfection makes you want to throw up.

Anyhow, a bunch of teks — that's short for Technical Security Guards — get out of the takvee. Six of them, all talking to each other in their implanted headsets. When they take up positions and give the all-clear, the takvee doors fold down, and out comes this proov. A female dressed in a shimmering white gown that you can almost see through but not quite. She's got beautiful gray sky–colored eyes, and perfect skin, and short hair that sort of glows, like the sun is always shining on her.

I'm staring at her. You can't help it with a proov. It makes me ache inside and feel scummy on the outside, like I should hide myself from her perfect eyes. But I don't hide — there's no place to go — and for some reason she notices me. Her hand goes up to her face and she touches her perfect ear. Communicating to the teks on her implant.

I'm thinking, run, boy, they're going to jolt you into a coma just for looking. But suddenly there's a tek close behind and I can't get away.

"Halt!" he goes, and I do. Like most teks, he's wearing a protective face mask, so I can't see his expression. Is he going to jolt me with his stunstik or what? I'm bracing myself for the buzz and hoping it won't set off spasms when he goes, "Follow me."

What he does is, he takes me to the proov. Which is like unheard of, a proov allowing a normal to approach. But that's what happens. And I can see the proov girl is young, maybe my age. Proovs don't wrinkle much, because of their genetically improved skin, but you can still tell whether they're young or old, if you get close enough. And this one is definitely young, maybe fourteen or fifteen. And her teeth are white, not yellow like normal teeth. I wonder if all proovs have white teeth. So perfectly white.

"Do you have a name?" she asks me.

I want to say, What do you think, just because we're not perfect, we don't have names? But all I can manage to get out of my choked-up throat is, "Spaz."

"Spaz," she says. Like she's tasting it on her tongue, and isn't sure if she likes it. "How odd. All of you seem to have such strange and interesting names down here in the latches." Then she points to one of the teks and goes, "Provide for him," and just like that she turns away and strides into the trade stall as if she's already forgotten that I exist.

Another tek pokes me in the back with a stunstik. The charge is set low so it doesn't knock me down or anything. "Stop staring, you!" he orders me. "Your eyes are dirty!"

There's nothing wrong with my eyes, but I do what he asks and stop looking at the beautiful proov while she goes trading. And the tek hands me a small plastic bag with edibles inside. Protein bars and carboshakes and choxbars and stuff like that. The way he does it makes me think the proov girl does this all the time: hands out goodies to normals, to make herself feel even more perfect than she already is.

I should hate her for that, for the way she feels, but I don't. I can't. You can't hate a proov when you're near one, because you want to be like them, you *ache* to be like them. You want to be perfect, too, and you know if you were improved you'd act just like they do, and feel what they feel, and glide through the world with sky-colored eyes and hair like sunlight, and nothing dirty or broken could ever touch you.

Then, when you'd had your little adventure in the

big bad dangerous Urb, you'd go home to Eden and live happily ever after.

Me, I go home to the Crypts.

My cube is small and dingy, with a chunk of foam on the floor, not a real bed, but it's way better than not having a place to sleep or just hang, even if the door doesn't lock from the inside.

That's a rule in the Crypts: no door locks, because the Bangers want to be able to enter anytime they feel like it. They take what they want, too, but for some reason they let me keep an old 3D, which is better than nothing. Nobody but me cares about watching 3Ds anymore, because why waste your time with a crummy hologram movie when you can boot up one of the brand-new mindprobes and see the whole show inside your head, like you were really there?

Anyhow, I toss the gummy's stuff in a corner and turn on the machine and start watching this 3D I've seen like ten thousand times. The one where Coley Riggins has to fight his way across the solar system, planet by planet, to rescue this gorgeous female who thinks he's dead, so she's going to marry this other guy, which would be a big mistake because the other guy is the one who keeps trying to kill poor Coley. You've probably seen it, if they still have the old 3Ds when you read this. If not, trust me, it's a really cool story, and usually I can get right into it and have fun pretending I'm as big and strong and good-looking as Coley Riggins, but today I can't concentrate on it. Instead, I keep thinking about the old geez, and what he said about those who will be alive at some future date.

For some reason the idea of "future" gets inside my head and won't let go. Future. That's like a time that doesn't exist yet. A world full of people who haven't been born yet, doing things that nobody's thought of yet.

Also I keep flashing on the proov girl with the sky-colored eyes, like somehow she's all mixed up with what happened in the stacks. Even though I know she doesn't have any connection to the old gummy they call Ryter.

I eat some of the stuff the proov girl gave me, which is better than the tasteless protein chunks you get from a food chute, but I can't stop thinking about Ryter, and how he said, *There are things about your life that are specific only to you. Secret things.*

What I don't understand is, how did he know? Does it have anything to do with that pile of scratch marks he calls a "book"?

There's one thing I do know: Sooner or later I'll have to go back to the stacks and find out.

CHAPTER FIVE

Three Rules for Billy Bizmo

I'M SOUND ASLEEP when the Bully Bangers invade my cube.

"Spaz! Spaz boy! Wake up!"

The Bangers are kicking through my stuff, checking out the goodies. One of them is pawing the edibles the proov girl gave me when Billy Bizmo smacks him. "Leave it!" Billy says, grinning at me. "You with us, Spaz boy? You with us or against us?"

"I'm with you," I say, trying to get my brain in gear.

I'd been deep inside this crazy, confusing dream about Coley Riggins rescuing the proov girl, or maybe the proov girl was rescuing him. Doesn't matter. What matters is paying attention to Billy Bizmo, because you never know what Billy is really thinking, and that's just one of about a thousand different things that makes him dangerous. Billy with his sharp, crooked nose, and curly hair like tufts of rusty iron, and his ratty yellow teeth, and the pale scars on his neck and jaw where somebody tried to kill him once and missed. Somebody no longer among the living, guaranteed.

"This junk come from the stacks?" he asks me, even though he already knows the answer. "That's all he had, the one they call Ryter? You sure he's not hiding nothing rich? Nothing special?"

"He's just an old gummy," I say. "That's all he had."

I can't believe I'm lying to Billy Bizmo, boss man of the Bangers. What do I care about the old man or his stupid pile of papers? But it's too late to take back the lie, and anyhow Billy seems more interested in the edibles.

"Explain," he says, holding up a carboshake.

So I tell him about the proov girl. How she came to the Maxi with her teks and told them to provide for me.

"Provide for you?" Billy says, fingering the scars on his neck as he mulls it over. "Why you, boy? Why you in particular?"

I shrug. "I was there, I guess."

"You mean this proov girl was looking for a char- ity case?"

"I dunno what a charity case is, Billy."

"Never mind. What did you say to her? Tell me exactly what you said."

"She asked me what they call me. I told her."

"And that's it? Your name?"

"That's it."

Billy crouches so he can study my eyes and see if I'm lying. That always makes me feel like I'm lying even when I'm telling the truth, which I am about the proov girl. The thing that makes Billy scary isn't his size, because he's not that much bigger than me. It's in his eyes. Sometimes his eyes are bright and interested and that makes you want to please him, and then he blinks and his eyes are dead and you're scared he wants to make you dead, too, just for the cool of it. Just because he can.

"Hmmm," he goes. "I've heard about this proov girl. She's a slummer. You know what a slummer is, Spaz? Huh?"

"No," I admit.

"A slummer is a proov who likes to mix with the rest of us. Gives 'em a thrill they can't find in Eden. You know what happens to a normal who gets mixed up with a proov, if the rest of the proovs find out?"

"No."

Billy makes a slicing sign across his throat. The idea seems to amuse him. "Forbidden, Spaz boy. They'll splash you. They'll cut your red. They'll blow you into particles. So keep away from the proov girl. You see her again, run like your life depends on it. Because it does. Do you believe me?"

"Yes."

"Good boy. Always believe Billy. That's rule number one. And what's rule number two?"

"Always obey Billy," I say.

"Excellent! Third rule?"

"Always speak true to Billy."

"Fantastic!" He's acting delighted with me, but I don't know if it's for real or a game he's playing. "Not bad for a spaz boy! Keep it up, kid! Follow Billy's rules and you may live to be as old as that gummy you ripped off." He hands me the proov girl's carboshake. "Go on," he says. "Enjoy. Have a taste of Eden."

A moment later they're gone and I'm alone in my cube. For some reason I'm shaking. No, not for some reason. Because I lied to Billy Bizmo. I broke his rules. If he finds out, he might decide to have me canceled, or he might decide to let me live but ban me from the Crypts. "Disfavor," they call it, which means you're on the curb, fending for yourself without protection or shelter.

Death or disfavor. I don't know which is worse, and I don't want to find out.

CHAPTER SIX

The Thing
About Bean

LATER THAT DAY I go back to the stacks. My plan is, I'll finish ripping off the old gummy and take his worthless papers, the junk he calls a book, and give it to Billy Bizmo, like I should have done in the first place. That's my plan, but in the end it doesn't work out that way.

This time Little Face pops up as soon as he sees me coming. "Choxbar!" he chirps, holding out his dirt-colored hands.

I go, "You know any other words? Huh?"

He shakes his head. "Chox! Chox!"

I get one out of my pouch and give it to him, and he gulps it down and holds out his hands again.

"You know the way," I tell him. "Take me to Ryter. Then you get another choxbar."

So Little Face guides me through the rows of

stackboxes like before, only this time the old gummy is standing in the door, waiting for me.

"Don't be surprised," he says with a smile. "Bad news travels fast in this part of the world."

I don't know why, but that hits me hard, the idea that I'm bad news. Of course it's true — me coming back to the stacks is bad news, what else could it be? But he looks so hopeful, like he's sure I'll prove him wrong, that my plan to rip him off again goes right out the back of my head.

Not today, I'm thinking, I'll steal his stupid "book" some other day.

"Come on in," Ryter says, stepping to one side. "Make yourself at home."

He's got this look in his watery old gray eyes, like he knows something I don't, but for some reason that doesn't make me mad. It just makes me want to know, too. But what, what is it he knows? He sees the look on my face and goes, "Something happened. Is it the Bangers? Have they canceled me?"

I shake my head. "Not yet."

"Not yet," he says, sounding real thoughtful. "Thank you for being honest with me. If you'd said 'nothing to worry about' I'd know it wasn't the truth. And I always want to know the truth."

Right, I'm thinking, just like Billy Bizmo.

Inside, it's cool and shadowy and of course there's no furniture, so I sit on the floor with my legs crossed. The old geez sits on the crate box he uses for a desk. The way light comes in, I can't see his face, and his baggy, old one-piece makes him look thin and shapeless at the same time, like he's lost inside his clothes.

"I've been thinking about you," Ryter says. "About your story."

"I told you," I say. "I don't have a story."

His head turns and now I can see his eyes, how big and old and kind they are. "What you're really saying is, you don't have a story worth telling," he says. "Let me be the judge of that."

I want to stand up and shout that he's got no right to tell me what I really mean — what makes him think he knows so much? — but instead I sit there and keep my mouth shut, maybe because underneath it all I know what he says is true.

"Start at the beginning," he suggests. "What's the first thing you remember?"

The first thing. That's easy. The first thing is when I got my little sister, Bean. The thing about Bean is, she isn't really my sister — we're not blood — but I didn't know that then, because I didn't know that Kay and Charly weren't my real mother and father.

All of that came later, when I started to grow, but when Bean came along I was maybe four years old, and that's the first thing I remember.

This tiny, widgy little face wrapped in a soft blanket. Her squinty eyes and her tiny little lips all smooched up like she'd been sucking a lemon. How she smelled like warm milk. Baby stuff — she was only a few days old, okay? But what I really remember is what happened when she saw me staring down at her. Her whole face smiled and her little hand came up and tried to grab my nose and that was it, I loved Bean right from that moment and it never changed. No matter what happened, all the bad things later, and me losing my family unit because of her, it never made me love Bean any less.

"So you were a foundling," Ryter says. "And Bean is your adoptive sister."

"Foundling?"

"An old word," he says, "but useful. Like you were found on the curb and taken in. Do you have any knowledge of your origins? Your birth mother? Father?"

I shrug like "Who cares?" because it doesn't matter. Nobody wants to claim a spaz boy, that's for sure.

"Never mind that part for now," Ryter says. "Tell me more about your sister. Tell me about Bean."

The thing that's really important to understand

about Bean is that she only sees the good in people, and never the bad. Because my foster dad, I suppose he's basically okay, but he's got this bad side, too, and Bean never saw it. Like she'd erased the idea of "bad" from her mind. So when everything blew up and Charly — that's his name, Charly — so when everything blew, and Charly got it fixed in his head that I was growing up dangerous and that somehow Bean might get infected with whatever it was that made me a spaz, Bean never saw it coming.

When Charly finally told me I had to leave, that he was banning me from the family unit, Bean tried to hug me and tell me it couldn't be true, he didn't mean it. Big mistake. Because Charly pulled her off me and smacked her right in the face and called her terrible names, names she didn't even understand, names no one should ever have to hear.

"What did Charly think?" Ryter wants to know. "Did he think you and Bean were luvmates?"

"I don't know what he thought," I say. "I'd never touch Bean that way, not ever. Even if she isn't blood she's still my little sister."

Ryter watches me for a while, like he's waiting for something to happen, for me to react, maybe. And then when I don't say anything more, he goes, "I wish I could say I'm surprised by your foster father's reaction. But the prejudice against epileptics is as old as the human race. Do you know the story of Alexander the Great?"

I shake my head.

"Remarkable man," Ryter says. "He conquered the world, a long long time ago."

"Yeah," I go. "So?"

"He had epilepsy, too. Many great humans have been epileptic. It's as if the brain compensates by increasing intelligence and ambition."

"Yeah, right."

"The epilepsy is part of what made you," he says. "Don't hate it."

Don't hate the spaz? Is he serious? The spaz is why I lost my family unit. Why I can never see Bean again. Why people run away when it happens. Spaz isn't just a name, it's a warning. Look out for the spaz boy, he might have a fit and bite you! He'll infect you! He'll infect your unborn children! Cast him out. Banish him. Disfavor him.

Cancel him, they sometimes whisper, *the boy is a monster, a mistake, he never should have been born.*

But Ryter, he doesn't get it. "You think of it as a curse," he says. "But the 'curse' is also a blessing. If you didn't have it you'd be sticking needles in your brain like all the others. Rotting your mind with probes. Living in a mindprobe instead of real life. You'd have trouble remembering what happened last week, never mind when you were four years old. You'd have forgotten all about your sister."

"Shut up!" I say, holding my hands to my ears. "Shut up!" But the stupid gummy won't shut up; he's trying to tell me something important even though I'm covering my ears and I don't want to hear it and I don't want to think about who I am or what's wrong with me or why I'm out here at the edge of the Urb, at the edge of the known world, listening to some old mope who's so crazy, he thinks about the future when everybody knows that the future doesn't exist.

"Shut up!" I scream. "Shut up!" And then I'm running away, running as fast as my feet will take me, running until I can't hear him anymore and the only word in my head is the word that never leaves, the word I hate the most, the word that means me.

Spaz, spaz, spaz.

CHAPTER SEVEN

All News
Is Bad News

WHEN I FINALLY slow down I'm a long way
from the stacks, in a part of the Urb I've never been
before. Where the streets are narrow and dark and the
buildings are so high, the sky disappears and it might
as well be night, even in the daytime. A place like
this, you stick to the shadows and try not to be seen,
because if they don't know you the locals will
assume you're enemy, and most of the time they're
right.

A drumfire burns on each street corner, and I can
see the enforcers warming their hands in the sooty
orange flames. They're the block guardians, armed
with chetty blades and probably splat guns, too.
They might know I'm almost down with the Bangers
and they might not. They might cut my red and they
might not. The "might" part will kill you, so I edge
my way along, trying to blend into the concrete.

I'm thinking, you mope, never go where you're not known. It's my own fault but I want to blame it on Ryter, for telling me things I don't want to hear.

This time I'm lucky. Nobody sees me. I creep away through the alleys, keeping to the darkest shadows, heart pounding so hard, my ears hurt. Barely breathing, moving as quiet as a whisper. Thinking, please let me get away, if I get away this time, I'll never be stupid again.

After what seems like forever I finally get to a place where I know the streets and they know me.

I made it, this time.

Back at the Crypts I'm ready to fall down on my foam and sleep, because being afraid makes you tired. But I never make it to the foam because someone is waiting inside my cube.

As soon as I step through the door, a voice hisses, "Don't move."

I can't see who it is because the power is out again, but the voice in the dark sounds as scared as me.

"Who is it?" I ask.

"Nobody," whispers the voice. "A runner."

A runner. Runners carry messages between the latches, crossing from one gang area to the next, and they're strictly forbidden. The gangs want to control everything, and that includes information. Because it's so dangerous — get caught and you're canceled —

latch runners are highly paid, and that's what bothers me: I don't know anyone who could afford to send me a message by runner. Or anyone who'd want to, even if they could.

"Shut the door!" the voice urges me.

I shut the door. The darkness is close and thick and makes me feel out of breath all over again.

"Show me your face," I demand, trying to sound brave.

"Never," says the voice. "Listen and listen well. I'm not here, we never met, understood? All I am is a message."

"What message?"

The runner's voice changes slightly, as he recites what he was sent to tell me. "I bring you news of home," he begins.

Already my heart is sinking because nobody knows better than me that all news is bad news. And this is the worst news there ever was.

"Your sister lies close to death," the runner tells me. "She wishes to see you one last time. End of message."

That's all. A moment later the door eases shut and I'm alone in my crib, in the dark. I find my old microflash and turn it on, but the light doesn't help.

Nothing helps. The words are like a scream inside my head that won't stop echoing.

Bean is dying and she wants to see me.

That's two impossible things. Bean can't be dying. And I can't see her because my old family unit lives on the other side of the Urb. That's why I was banished to Billy Bizmo's latch, so there'd be some distance between us. Now if I want to get to Bean — and I do, more than anything — I'll have to go through at least three warring latches that won't let a stranger pass. Unless.

"Billy Bizmo," I say to myself, and the name gives me hope. Hope to see Bean, hope to save her somehow.

Billy might grant me safe passage. He has the power. If he wants to make it happen. Maybe he can even fix whatever it is that's wrong with Bean.

I'm not thinking too clear; there's no room for anything inside my brain but what to do about Bean. Or else I might have remembered another of Billy's rules. The rule that you never go to him, he has to come to you. Because when I get to the bottom level of the Crypts, where the Bangers have their headquarters, the enforcers throw me down on the damp concrete.

"Search him," I hear someone say, and rough hands go over every inch of me, looking for weapons.

"He's clean."

They flip me over so I'm looking up into their laser sights.

"State your purpose, scum."

"Billy," I gasp, closing my eyes so the lasers don't burn me. "Need to see Billy."

"Billy don't need to see you."

"It's the spaz boy," one of them says. "Must be having a fit, to come down here without an invite."

"Crazy mope. Let's cut him."

I figure they'll do it, they'll cut me for sure, but for some reason they hold off. Now they're mumbling to each other, but I can't make out the words.

"Do it," someone says. "Go on and slam the little mope."

Boots womp into my ribs so hard, the air goes out of me and won't come back in.

"Move and you die."

I'm making this can't breathe noise, erp, erp, and it makes them laugh and go, listen to the spaz boy, he's singing our song. I'm not thinking of anything except finding a way to make my lungs work. Finally the air whistles into me and their steel-toed boots prod at me like I'm a bug that can't turn over, which is pretty close to the truth.

"Pick 'im up."

They carry me into another room. A room where

the light is dim and purple and the air smells of incense and candles and something like medicine.

Billy Bizmo's private crib. I don't care how much it hurt, I'm in. They drop me on a rug at his feet and tell me not to move, not to say a word, because the boss man is busy, he's got things on his mind.

When my eyes adjust to the dim purple light I see what they're talking about. The thing on Billy's mind is a needle. He's probing. That's the medicine smell, the disinfectant for the electrode needle that slips into his brain.

The boss man of the Bangers sits in a big, padded chair, like the throne of a mighty king in the backtimes. His eyes are open but you can tell he's not seeing the room, or the candles all around, or me. He's seeing whatever is happening inside his head, where the mindprobe is playing. Putting him right there, like he's inside a moving hologram only better. Better than real. Better than anything.

Not that I know from personal experience. Like I said at the beginning, a spaz like me can't probe. They say it's like entering another world, a world created for your pleasure and excitement, a world where all your dreams come true and every wish is granted. A world much, much better than the one we live in, that's for sure.

If I could do it I'd probe myself into a place where

I still lived with my family unit, and we were all happy and healthy and loved one another, forever and ever, like in Eden. But I can't probe and I can't wait until Billy comes out of it, either, because Bean needs me.

So I do something incredibly stupid: I put my hand on Billy's ankle and try to shake him awake. At first nothing happens, and then all at once he comes back to life. He grabs my hair with one hand and sticks a splat gun in my face.

His terrible dark voice goes, "Who disturbs me? Who dares make Billy unhappy?"

I'm too scared to speak. I've seen what his gun can do, and how it got its name.

"Speak," says Billy. "Speak to me, or the last sound you hear will be 'splat.'"

"It's me," I say. "Spaz."

"Impossible," Billy says, pressing the gun into my forehead as he slides back the trigger guard. "The spaz boy is too frightened to show his face down here. You're an impostor."

"My sister," I tell him. "My sister is sick. I have to see her."

"You lie. The spaz boy has no sister."

"We're not blood, but she's still my sister."

He's staring at me as if I'm not quite real, as if

I'm something that came from the probe he was watching. But then his eyes sort of flicker and I know he recognizes me. Slowly he takes the splat gun away from my forehead. "It *is* you," he says. "What happened to give you courage?"

"Bean," I say. "I heard she was sick."

He thinks about it, then shrugs. "Most unfortunate. But as you say, this girl is no blood of yours."

"She asked for me," I tell him. "They live on the other side of the Urb. I need your help. I need safe passage."

I beg, I plead, but Billy Bizmo sits like a stone, a cold stone with dead eyes. He could care less what I want, or if Bean lives or dies. There will be no safe passage, and I am forbidden to leave.

"Hear me, Spaz boy," he says. "No one leaves my latch without my permission, and that includes you. Too bad for your little friend, but people die every day. Every hour. Every minute. So put it out of your mind. There's nothing you can do about it."

"Billy, please."

He places the splat gun under my nose. "Billy says no," he whispers. "If you ask again, you die. Is that clear?"

"Yes, Billy."

"Good," he says. "Now, what are the rules?"

"Always believe Billy. Always obey Billy. Always speak true to Billy."

"Most excellent," he says. "Again."

By his command I repeat his rules, believe, obey, speak true, but inside my head I'm already running away.

CHAPTER EIGHT

The Smell of Lightning

ONCE WHEN SHE WAS eight years old, Bean almost died. They said she had the bone marrow sickness, and her blood was so weak, it couldn't keep her alive. Her eyes had this going away look, and all she could do was lie on her bed and tremble. She couldn't eat or sleep, and everything hurt, from her skin all the way down into her bones.

Nothing helped until this old woman came, a healer. The healer passed her hands over Bean and said she might live or she might die, but the only thing that might save her was a special remedy to strengthen her blood.

The remedy was this gooey liquid stuff that smelled awful and tasted worse, and I was the only one who could get Bean to take it. If her mom or dad tried to spoon it into her mouth, she'd spit it out. But for me she'd make a face and swallow the stuff. She was too weak to speak, so I'd tell her these dumb little stories I made up, about how she was always stopping me from doing stupid things, which was pretty close to the truth, and sometimes she'd smile and doze off for a little while.

For the whole time she was sick I stayed with her, and slept on the floor by her bed, because I had this weird idea that if I ever left her side she wouldn't be there when I got back. It scared me worse than her dying, that she might just disappear. Charly said it was unnatural, my not wanting to leave her room, but Kay, my foster mom, said, Let the boy be, can't you see he makes her smile?

Then one morning when I woke up and looked over, Bean was sleeping peacefully and the color was back in her cheeks. Either the remedy worked or Bean had gotten better on her own. I was so happy, it felt like my head would explode, and then when I ran to tell everyone the good news I must have got so excited, it brought on a seizure. I remember shouting, "She's better! She's better!" and then it hit me and the blackness rose up.

When I came out of it my foster mom said it was true, Bean was much better, but Charly said, "That's it, he's not going into her room anymore; what if he pitched a fit and hurt our little girl?" From that day Charly always looked at me different, as if I'd turned into someone he didn't know, even though they'd raised me almost since I was born.

None of that matters now, not what Charly thinks, or me losing my family unit, or anything. The only important thing is how to get to Bean so I can make her take the remedy. I don't care how many times she spits it out, I'll just keep trying until she makes a funny face and swallows the stuff.

So I go back to my crib, throw a few things in my carrybag, fill my pockets with the goodies the proov girl gave me, and head out before anyone tries to stop me.

One thing I know for sure: There's no way to get through the main part of the latch. The Bangers are everywhere, and they'll be on the lookout for me, to make sure I don't disobey Billy's orders.

My only chance is out along the Edge.

Night falls before I get there, which means I have to find my way through the stacks in the dark. I don't want to waste the power in my microflash because there'll be no place to recharge it, not where I'm going. So I stumble along, bumping into piles of old bricks and junk so useless, even the stackboxers threw it away. Trying to remember where the Pipe is from here, because the old water pipe points to the Edge.

A few small fires glow near the stacks, probably

fired up to keep the wild dogs away. I'd love to warm my hands over the flames and rest for a while, but there's no time for taking my ease, not until I get clear of Billy's latch.

As I turn to go, Little Face finds me in the dark. "Chox!" he cries, and hugs my leg.

When my heart finally comes unstuck from my throat, I go, "Don't you know it's dangerous out here? Where do you live? Who looks out for you?" but all the little guy will say is chox, chox, so what choice do I have?

I give him my last choxbar and take his hand and walk him toward the fires, hoping the stack people will know where he belongs. I'm also hoping that old geez Ryter won't be there, because he'll want to talk about Bean and that's the last thing I need right now. Talking won't help — I have to get to her.

The people tending the fire back away, blending into the shadows, waiting for me to make a move. When they see Little Face holding my hand, a few of them come forward, showing off crude chetty blades made from the rusted steel wreckage that lies all around the stackboxes. Mostly the 'boxers look ragged and broke down somehow, as if they always expect to lose, and even though the odds are ten to one, they seem to be more scared of me than I am of them, which is just fine with me.

"Go away!" this one old woman screeches. "Leave the boy alone!"

"Stand down," I say, raising up my hands. "I brought the kid back, understand? Now I'll be on my way."

Little Face finishes the choxbar and prances around by the fire, grinning and spoofing without saying a word. No one comes forward to claim him, but he seems to know the people there.

Then as I turn to go, a voice pipes up. "Who you going to bustdown this time, Banger? Another old gummy?"

I figure, don't even turn around. Just keep going, before the darkness gives them courage and they decide to charge me with their rusty old chetty blades.

"Look at him go, the big bad Bully Banger!" crows the taunting voice. "He ain't so brave at night, is he? None of his gang to help him now, is there?"

I can hear them moving behind me but I don't look back. I'm thinking, you blew it, you mope, you ripped them off and then came back alone, in the dark, what did you expect?

"Get him!" somebody yells. "Cut his red!"

Most days I can outrun just about anybody, but this isn't most days, it's the darkest part of the night and the ground is strange under my feet. Almost before I get going something trips me hard, and suddenly I'm flat on my face, surrounded.

"Don't let him get away!"

"Bust him down and see how he likes it!"

They're all around me but keeping their distance, as if afraid that I'll strike back. Maybe they think I've got a splat gun hidden in my carrybag, or a stunstik or something. If they knew all I had was an old microflash and a few edibles, they'd swarm over me in an instant.

"Cut his red! Cut his red!" shouts the 'boxer who started it. He's hanging back, this scrawny mope with a scraggly beard and crazy burning eyes. Even in the dark I can see the spit flying out of his mouth as he screams for them to cut me.

"Get up!" another of them shouts.

I get slowly to my feet, holding my hands to show I haven't any weapons. I'm trying to think of what to say that will make them let me go when a terrible feeling starts to come over me.

"No," I say to myself. "Please, not now."

But I can't keep it from happening, no matter how hard I try. It always begins this way. First the smell of lightning fills my nose, the clean electric smell of the air after a thunderstorm, and then the blackness rises up and takes me down.

When I come out of it, Ryter is there, holding a damp cloth to my forehead. I'm in his stackbox.

They must have carried me here — I certainly didn't walk.

"You're okay," he tells me. "It's over."

Like always I'm exhausted and weak and ashamed. I hate it when someone sees me like this.

"A grand mal seizure," Ryter says. "Very impressive. I tried to put a stick between your teeth, and you bit it in half."

That explains my sore teeth. I have that familiar dreamy feeling that always comes afterward, and more than anything I want to sleep and forget. But then it comes back to me, like a splash of cold water on my brain, and I sit up and say, "I've got to go. What hour is it?"

"The hour before dawn," Ryter says. "What's your hurry?"

I'm trying to stand up but my legs are too weak to make it.

"Rest," he says and, old as he is, Ryter easily holds me down. He doesn't understand why I can't stay, so I tell him about Bean and how I have to leave before Billy Bizmo reaches out and stops me.

Ryter listens, and his ancient eyes go soft. Then he nods and says, "Ah. Now it all makes sense."

I'm not sure that anything makes sense, but I haven't got the strength to argue. Tired, so tired.

"Sleep," he urges me. "We leave at dawn."

I fight to stay awake but my eyes close on their own and in three deep breaths I'm fast asleep.

When the old man wakes me, the sky is pale gray and so low you can almost reach out and touch it.

"Time to go," he says, nudging my shoulder. "The Bangers are looking for you."

That startles me wide awake.

"How do you know?" I ask.

He shrugs. "I told you before, bad news travels fast out here near the Edge. Have you recovered? Are you ready?"

He's got a ragged old sack strapped to his back, and a long, crooked stick to help him walking.

"You can't come with me," I tell him.

"And why is that?"

"You'll slow me down. I have to move fast."

Ryter raises his walking stick and pokes me in my stomach hard enough to get my attention. "Listen, young fool. We haven't much time, so I won't waste any of it being polite. I already saved your life once. That little mob would have torn you apart if I hadn't intervened. So what happens the next time you have a seizure and no one's there to keep you safe?"

I shove the stick away. "I'll take care of myself."

His tone softens. "Think about it, son. You can't do this thing alone. Cross three latches without a guide? You'll be dead before sundown, or wish you were."

I'm shrugging on my carrybag, edging to the door of his miserable little stackbox. "What do you care? Why do you want to help me?"

The old man raises his stick and bars the door, like he's buying time while he thinks about his answer. "Two reasons," he says after a pause. "First, I want to know how your story ends. And second, this will be my last opportunity for great adventure. A mission to save the life of a beloved young woman — what more could an old man want? I shall accompany you, and then write our tale of courage in my book."

"You're crazy," I warn him. "You might be killed."

"Crazy?" He laughs and shakes his head. "They said Don Quixote was crazy, too."

"Who's Don Keehote?" I ask.

"A man who believed in doing the right thing, even if it cost him his life," Ryter says. He shoves me out the door. "Come on, boy. Let me show you the way."

And he marches into the daylight with his puny walking stick raised like a mighty sword.

CHAPTER NINE

By the Edge We Travel, By the Edge We Live or Die

LITTLE FACE TRIES TO FOLLOW us. He's running along, leaping from one junk pile to the next, making a game of it. "Chox!" he sings out. "Chox!"

He knows I haven't got any more. It's like he gets as much pleasure out of saying the word as eating the actual choxbar.

"You made a friend," Ryter says, grinning at me.

But he knows the little boy can't come with us, that it's much too dangerous. He signals to Little Face and the kid dances up to him. Ryter has a word in his ear. A moment later the kid sings, "Chox!" one last time and then runs back in the direction of the stacks.

It's a relief but at the same time I'm already sort of missing the little pest.

"There are thousands like him," Ryter comments

as we pick up our pace. "Orphaned or abandoned, fending for themselves. Very few live to be as old as you, let alone as ancient as me. A great writer once wrote of a very similar situation, in a city called London. His name was Charles Dickens, and he, too, was an epileptic."

That's it. I stop in my tracks. Ryter looks at me with concern. "Something wrong?" he asks.

"Shut up about the spaz, okay? I don't want to hear about it. I don't want to talk about it."

"And you don't want to think about it," Ryter adds. "Fine. Agreed. I shall not speak of the innumerable famous and successful human beings who shared your condition. I shall not speak of Julius Caesar, Napoléon Bonaparte, Leonardo da Vinci, Agatha Christie, Lewis Carroll, or Harriet Tubman. I will never again mention Joan of Arc, Vincent van Gogh, Sir Isaac Newton, Alfred Lord Tennyson, Edgar Allan Poe, or the great Paganini. Done. Finished. My lips are zipped." The old man looks really pleased with himself and then gestures with his walking stick. "Proceed. Lead on."

I go, "I thought *you* knew the way."

He shrugs. "This is your mission. Have you a plan?"

"You know I don't."

"Ah," he says. "Then may I suggest we travel by the Pipe?"

Like I mentioned before, the Pipe runs out to the edge of the known world, and keeps on going. They say it runs all the way into the Badlands, where the radiation will rot your bones. But what I didn't know until Ryter tells me is that parts of the Pipe branch off and run between the latches.

"All part of the greatest water supply system ever devised," he says, leading us under the ruins of the giant pipe, which is supported by crumbling concrete pylons. "A masterpiece of hydraulic engineering," he says. "It would still be functional, except the main source of water dried up after the Big Shake. They tried various other solutions for a century or so, at enormous expense, but nothing worked out, and in the long run it fell into disrepair."

He loves to rattle on with all his backtimer talk, and I'm willing to listen if he can really help me find Bean. And he's right about the Pipe. I have to help him climb up the side of the pylon because the old iron stairs are partly rusted away, and when we get to the Pipe itself, you can see where one of the access panels has been unbolted.

"There," says Ryter. "Whew! I was a much younger man the last time I climbed this high. Go on, check it out."

I slip through the opening. There's plenty of room

to stand up inside, if you don't mind being ankle deep in smelly old rainwater. Shafts of light come through where bolts have rusted out, and it makes the whole Pipe look shot full of bullet holes. "Hey!" I shout, and my voice sounds like it echoes all the way to the next latch.

Ryter crawls into the Pipe and sits panting, out of breath.

"You'll never make it," I tell him. "We've got miles and miles to go."

"I'll make it," he gasps. "I've got a book to finish."

I stare at him huddled there, his frayed leggings soaking up the puddle of rainwater. "No one cares about your old book!" I tell him. "Let's go."

"Right," he says, using his walking stick to get himself standing.

"Ready?" I say, feeling bad for yelling at the old gummy.

"Ready as I'll ever be." He looks around and seems to like what he sees. "By the Edge we travel, son. By the Edge we live or die."

He makes everything sound so noble and grand, but the truth is we're a couple of nobodies hiding inside a rusty old water pipe. Just us and the pale rats that scurry ahead. We slop along in the dead water for a while and then we come to a part that's dry underfoot, which is easier going. Ryter is breathing better now and he looks stronger than I would have thought possible.

Maybe he'll make it after all.

"Seven miles, more or less," he says, keeping up with me. "That'll bring us to the next latch."

"You've done this before?" I ask.

"Oh yes," he says. "Years ago. Certain people took a dislike to me and I thought it best to move along. Many refugees used the Pipe in those days, to move around the city. Now it seems to have been forgotten, like so many other things."

We plod on. There's nowhere to go but straight ahead. Small red eyes watch us, keeping their distance. I'm not afraid of rats, not while I'm awake. Sleeping, that's different. They say a rat will eat your nose before you can wake up. Eat it before you can smell them. Teeth so sharp you don't feel a thing until too late.

"Why do the Bangers care if you leave?" Ryter wants to know.

I explain what Billy said, about how no one could go anywhere without his permission.

"What I don't understand is why the gang leader focused on you in particular," Ryter says.

I shrug and say, "He took an interest."

"Exactly," Ryter says, nodding to himself. "But why?"

I can tell he doesn't expect me to come up with an answer, that he's really asking himself. But it borks me off that he thinks I'm not important enough to matter.

Ryter sees the look on my face and gives my arm a reassuring squeeze. "Something to ponder, son. I mean no disrespect. But sometimes it can be useful, not to say life-saving, to understand why a latchboss does what he does. I've an idea that Mr. Bizmo knows something we don't. He had a specific reason for forbidding your departure. If we can figure out what it is, it may help us get where we're going."

"Yeah? That's what you think?" I say. "Well, here's what I think. Trying to read Billy's mind will get us canceled."

That shuts the old geez up, and we trudge along in silence for a couple of miles. We come to a part of the Pipe that sags, which means the rainwater has collected knee-high. The water is slimy and buzzing with mosquitoes, but Ryter doesn't hesitate, he wades through it like he could care less about the wet or the bugs or the slithery things that slip along the edges. The weirdest thing about him, though, is how he doesn't seem to get mad at me when I'm mad at him. Like he expects me to be borked about stuff and doesn't take it personally.

Later on, when we stop to rest for a few minutes, I share some of the edibles with him. He looks the stuff over and goes, "This is proov food, right?" so I tell him about the proov girl and he says, "Dangerous. Contact with the genetically improved is exceedingly dangerous. Not for them. For us. We're what they used to be, and they hate us for it."

He eats the proov food, though, every crumb, and then we're on our way. We walk and walk until the daylight fades and the darkness makes the Pipe seem even bigger and longer, and the red eyes are closer. We walk until we feel wind in our faces, and that's when Ryter stops and says, "We've come to the break."

"The break?"

"A section of the Pipe is missing up ahead. We'll have to go to ground for a mile or so."

I walk out to where the Pipe ends, but it's so dark, I can't see all the way to the ground. It feels like we're floating in the sky and that makes me dizzy, so I back carefully away, until the rusty steel is more or less solid under my feet.

"How do we get down?" I ask.

"We better wait until daylight," Ryter suggests.

"No sense coming this far and then breaking our necks, is there?"

It drives me crazy not to keep moving, but I know he's right about waiting. I can't save Bean if I'm busted up, that's for sure. So we crouch at the curve of the Pipe and take turns trying to sleep.

"You go first," he says. "I'll entertain our little friends."

He tosses a pebble at the red eyes and they scurry back out of range.

"Pleasant dreams," he says, and I'm thinking, right, like I'm really going to fall asleep in a rat-filled pipe, but the next thing I know he's shaking me and whispering, "Wake up. They're coming."

I hear it.

shika-tik-tik, shika-tik-tik

The sound gets closer and closer. Something is coming down the Pipe to get us.

CHAPTER TEN

Attack of
the Monkey Boys

SHIKA-TIK-TIK, shika-tik-tik

I'd give anything for a chetty blade or a splat gun, but all I've got is my carrybag. Better than nothing, but just barely. It has a rope loop on it, so I can swing it when the thing comes within range. "Thing" because it doesn't sound human. Too delicate and steady to be the Bangers. Too large and loud to be a rat.

Unless it's a rat the size of a wild dog. Just thinking about that makes me shrink up inside myself.

Ryter and me are both hugging the curved wall of the Pipe, in hopes that whatever it is will go right by us.

shika-tik . . . tik

No such luck — it's slowing down.

I'm staring into the dark so hard, it feels like my

eyes are bugging out. *Tik . . . tik . . .* closer and closer, until it sounds like I could reach out and touch it. Or it could reach out and touch me.

The shadows move, and I see it has the shape of a hunched-up monster. It spots me or senses me somehow and veers in my direction. *Tik . . . tik* must be talons dragging. Claws as sharp as needles. Icy water floods through my guts. My heart slams. I've forgotten how to breathe. The thing is reaching out for me.

I rear back with the carrybag and start to swing with all my strength.

"Chox," the monster says.

Just what we need tagging along, a five-year-old kid who only knows one word. What happened is Little Face found himself a walking stick like Ryter's and dragged it along, *shika-tik-tik.* We're stuck with him because there isn't time to take him back, or anybody there to keep him even if we did. It seems like no matter what I do, the kid keeps finding me in the dark.

I figure it's the gummy's fault somehow.

"If you hadn't come along, the little brat would still be there," I tell him.

"You're the one who fed him," Ryter says. "The poor child has been hungry all his life, so it's no wonder he's fastened on you, Mr. Choxbar."

The gummy speaks true, but that doesn't make me any less angry. Why should I care what happens to the little brat if nobody else does?

"Don't be discouraged," Ryter says. "The child can look out for himself. That's how he survives."

"Running a latch is hard enough alone," I remind him. "With three it's impossible."

"Oh," says Ryter, raising his feathery white eyebrows. "So you're an experienced latch runner, are you?"

The way he looks at me makes me want to tell the truth.

"I've never left the latch," I admit. "Not since they brought me here."

"Then perhaps you'll take my word for it. What we're attempting to do is far from impossible. Dangerous, yes. But hardly impossible. After all, a runner crossed three latches to get the message to you, didn't he? If he can do it, so can we. And with three of us we're less likely to be mistaken for professional runners or smugglers."

What he says makes sense, although I hate to admit it. I'm out of choxbars, but I give Little Face a chunk of proov edibles and he gobbles it down like he's starving, flashing a smile that eats up his whole face.

We wait until the sky is all the way light, and then

check out the end of the Pipe. There's no stairway, but Ryter figures we can skinny down the pylon somehow. "We haven't much choice," he says. "We'll have to risk it."

As it turns out, Little Face shows us the way. He slips over the Edge and then crawls down, using the rusty steel bars that stick out of the concrete. About ten seconds later he's standing on the ground below, shouting, "Chox! Chox!" which I guess is his name for me, or maybe just a way of saying, *I did it!*

Ryter's saggy old face is pale and worried, but I know better than to say anything. He goes next, and it takes him a lot longer than Little Face, but he manages to get down without breaking any bones.

Now they're both looking up at me. "Come on!" Ryter calls out. "You can do it!"

I think about Bean, how she's waiting for me, and how it doesn't matter if I'm scared of heights. About halfway down, my feet slip and I have to hug the concrete to keep from falling. Don't move, I'm thinking, if you move, you fall.

"You're almost there," Ryter says, right below me. "Reach down with your right foot."

I do what he says and he keeps telling me where to put my feet and after about a thousand years I make it all the way to the ground and stand there shaking.

"What if the spaz had hit me?" I say, more to my-self than anybody else.

"It didn't," Ryter says. "And we don't have time to worry about things that didn't happen. We better get a move on; it's a two-hour hike to the next section of the Pipe. Assuming it's still there."

"What?" I say with a gasp. "You don't know?"

"The last time I came this way was many years ago," he admits. "Things change. You never know a thing for certain until you've seen it with your own eyes."

What I do see is pretty amazing. In this latch the old scrapers come all the way out to the Edge. They say in the backtimes the scrapers were made of glass. Giant glass buildings a hundred stories high, maybe more. They say people went inside the glass build-ings, traveling up and down in electric boxes, and that toward the end the people never came out or walked on the ground, but lived and died inside. The scrapers are just twisted steel skeletons now, enor-mous, eerie-looking things that disappear some-where up in the smog.

Tons and tons of crumbled concrete surround the base of each scraper, stuff that must have fallen when the Big Shake rocked the world and split open the earth and dried up the rivers and stuff. When the light hits it the wreckage glitters like diamonds, but Ryter says that's only chunks of broken glass, and that many a man has died looking for treasure that doesn't exist.

"The only real treasure is inside your head," he says, tapping the side of his skull. "Memories are better than diamonds, and nobody can steal them from you."

Staring up at the scrapers makes me feel extra small. "Why did they build them so high?" I ask him.

"Because they could, I guess."

"But weren't they afraid of earthquakes?"

"Not afraid enough," he says. "I don't suppose anybody really knows how bad a thing can be until it actually happens."

The sun is barely visible through the smog, but Ryter says if we keep it over our left shoulders and walk straight ahead, we'll get where we're going, no problem. We trudge along for a couple of hours and in all that time we don't see another living thing. No weeds, no insects, nothing. Just ruins melting into dead sand. Not even the rats are dumb enough to live this close to the Edge, which is fine with me.

We seem to be alone, but I keep getting this creepy feeling that something is watching us. Maybe the scrapers themselves. I don't know if the old buildings can see or not, but they sure can moan when the wind goes through the steel. Moaning like they know they're slowly dying and can't do anything about it.

As it turns out, the Pipe is right where Ryter thought it was. Sitting up there on its crumbling pylons, ready to take us where we're going.

We're almost there when the howling starts.

"Ah-hee-hoo-hoo! Ah-hoo-yip-yip!"

It sounds like wild animals, but somehow I know it isn't, not exactly. Little Face hugs my leg. I can feel him shivering, which scares me almost as much as the howling.

"Ah-hee-hoo-hoo! Ah-hoo-yip-yip!"

They come pouring out of the ruins, howling and scampering and waving their arms.

"Monkey Boys," says Ryter. "Don't move."

They swarm in, surrounding us, and I can see their faces painted to look like monkeys, and their wild eyes that want to kill us.

CHAPTER ELEVEN

Mongo
the Magnificent

MONKEY BOYS. I've heard of them. Monkey Boys control this latch like the Bully Bangers control theirs. But the creatures pouring out of the ruins no longer act human; they've become as wild as the paint on their faces. And it isn't only the face paint — their teeth have been sharpened into fangs, and their fingernails are like yellowed, curving claws.

"Something's wrong!" Ryter hisses to me.

"No kidding!" I hiss right back at him.

As the crazy clawed hands reach out to grab us, Ryter twists around and looks me in the eye. "Do not resist," he warns. "They'll tear us limb from limb."

I figure that may happen anyway, but fighting won't do any good: There's way too many of them and not enough of us. I try to keep hold of Little Face, but as the swarm lifts us he gets separated. The little guy yells, "Chox! Chox!" and it means *help me!* but I can't help him or Ryter or myself because we're being carried away by a hundred howling madmen with ferocious snapping fangs.

I'm thinking the Bangers never act like this, not even when they're canceling a victim, but the Monkey Boys don't seem to have a leader making rules and telling them what to do. The old gummy's right — something *is* wrong. The Monkey Boys don't just look like animals and act like animals — they've *become* animals.

The screaming swarm carries us back into the ruins, under the long steel shadows of the giant scrapers, to a place where the air smells of blood and rust.

They bring us to a strange dark structure, a fortress made from the iron bones of a fallen building. Great iron beams hammered into the ground and bound together with woven steel cable. Splat guns and cannons stick from slots in the walls. The swarm of wild Monkey Boys surrounds the fort, leaping and howling, *ah-hee-hoo-hoo, ah-hee-yip-yip!*

The howling becomes a word.

"Mongo!" they howl. "Mongo! Mongo! Mongo!"

They keep screaming for Mongo until a section of the great iron wall is lowered by cable, and we are carried into the fort. The entire swarm tries to get inside, but a squad of teks is guarding the fort, and the teks hold their ground, chopping at the mob with chetty blades and stunstiks, driving them back.

The Monkey Boys drop us to the dirt and back away. The great door is raised behind us, shutting out the swarm, and for the first time since we've been seized, the howling stops.

For some reason the quiet is even more terrifying.

The teks point their weapons at us and indicate that we get up.

Ryter can barely stand, but he waves me off when I try to help him. "Show neither aggression nor fear," he whispers to me urgently. "Just play along."

Play along? I've no idea what the old man is talking about. How do you play along with a dozen armored thugs who communicate by grunts? The best I can do is keep Little Face close by as the teks herd us deeper into the fortress.

The smell is terrible and gets worse. No plumbing, obviously. Very little power, because the lights keep flickering. Whoever is in charge of this place, he's not paying attention, that's for sure.

We pass a stockade crammed with prisoners who stare at us with dead eyes. They're all bone thin, wearing tattered rags. They don't even have the strength to moan or beg for help or keep themselves clean.

"A good sign," Ryter says out of the side of his mouth.

A good sign? The old gummy must be losing it. But then I realize what he's getting at. If they keep prisoners, that means their victims aren't canceled immediately. Which means we might have a chance to survive, at least for a while.

The teks shove us down dark, winding passageways, and we make so many turns, there's no way I could find my way back, even if we did manage to escape.

As it turns out, we hear Mongo before we see him. A loud voice booms through the passageway: "HEAR MONGO AND OBEY . . . HEAR MONGO AND OBEY . . . ," over and over, like an old 3D stuck on replay.

Which, as it turns out, is pretty close to the truth.

When we get closer to the booming voice, lights begin to glow, reflecting off the walls. Then at last we turn the corner and there he is.

"To your knees!" the tek boss shouts, shoving us down with his stunstik. "Pay homage to Mongo the Magnificent! Hear him and obey!"

We drop to our knees and look up at Mongo. He's a fierce, powerful-looking latchboss with bright, blazing eyes, huge, muscular arms, shoulder-length hair the color of midnight, and a snarling, blood-red monkey tattooed on his enormous chest. He thumps the tattoo with his fists and goes, "HEAR MONGO AND OBEY . . . HEAR MONGO AND OBEY."

It's crazy, but I almost laugh out loud. Mongo the Magnificent is nothing more than a hologram. A short loop from a 3D, repeating over and over again. It wouldn't fool a two-year-old kid, and it doesn't fool me.

Ryter murmurs, "I'm going to try something. Whatever you do, don't interfere."

Before I can stop him, the old gummy stands up slowly, leaning on his stick.

"On your knees!" the tek boss commands. "Homage to Mongo!"

All the weapons aim at Ryter. It's hard to tell with the masks they wear, but the teks look nervous, uncertain.

"You must take us to the real Mongo!" Ryter tells them, raising his voice to be heard over the sound of the repeating hologram.

"Knees!" cries the tek boss. "Homage!" But he sounds uncertain.

"Does Mongo live?" Ryter demands.

"Mongo lives," says the tek boss. He sounds puzzled, as if he's not quite sure why he's talking to the old gummy instead of canceling him.

Ryter walks up to the tek boss. I'm sure he's about

to die, but the tek boss doesn't move. "Take off the mask," Ryter suggests. "Let me see your face."

Much to my amazement, the tek boss takes off his armored security mask. Under the mask he's just another young guy with a round face and worried eyes, and he's looking at Ryter like he can't decide, should he listen to the old man or cut his red.

"You must take us to Mongo," Ryter tells him. "Maybe we can help."

The tek boss hesitates, and his face gets all wrenched up like he's in pain. "I don't have the authority."

"Does anyone have the authority?" Ryter gently asks. "No? I thought not. Think about it, son. What would Mongo want you to do?"

"Hear him and obey," the tek boss responds instantly.

"Yes, of course," Ryter says patiently. "And you've done a splendid job of obeying him, under very difficult circumstances. Keeping your squad together, defending the fort, and so on. But now you must do more. You must help Mongo. Take us to him."

"I-I-I'm afraid," the tek boss stammers.

"We're all afraid," Ryter says soothingly. "If the situation continues, the fort will be overwhelmed and you'll all be destroyed. I think you know that. Something must be done."

The tek boss speaks uneasily, as if afraid of being overheard. "What you say is true. But what would you have us do?"

"Let's start with trying to help Mongo, shall we?" Ryter suggests.

The poor tek boss looks like he's being tortured, but finally he nods and goes, "Follow me. But if we all die, don't say I didn't warn you."

"Warning acknowledged," Ryter says. "Now proceed."

It's one of the most amazing things I've ever witnessed: an old gummy — an intruder into the latch — persuading a tek boss to disobey his orders. When I look at Ryter it's like he knows what I'm thinking, because he gives me a wink and makes it clear that we just go along while we've got the chance.

"Chox?" Little Face asks, tugging at my leg.

"Sssh," I tell him. "We'll be okay."

And for the first time since the Monkey Boys grabbed us, I really do think we might make it out alive. Of course I'm assuming Ryter intends to overpower the young tek boss when we get the chance, and then shoot our way out of the fortress. As it turns out, he's got an entirely different plan: The crazy old fool really does want to see Mongo — the real one, not the hologram version.

We follow the frightened tek boss into a much

smaller passageway — barely room to move, really — and then up a set of metal ladder steps.

At the top of the stairs the tek boss glances furtively around, takes a deep breath, and then wrenches open the lock on an overhead hatch. He gives Ryter a mournful look, then cautiously pushes open the hatch.

"Inside," he whispers.

Without hesitation Ryter climbs up the last few rungs of the ladder and disappears through the hatch.

What choice do I have? I follow him inside, into the secret lair of Mongo the Magnificent, boss man of the Monkey Boys.

CHAPTER TWELVE

The Problem
with Looping

THE FIRST THING I notice is the horrible
stink. Think of moldy dead rats and rotten eggs and
dirty diapers. This is worse, much worse. After crawl-
ing up through the hatch, I roll to one side and wait
for my eyes to adjust to the glittery dimness. Except
for the stink, it reminds me of Billy Bizmo's place,
only bigger. A latchboss pleasure-crib stuffed with
goodies and gizmos and every possible gaming
device. There are lots of soft inflatos that mold
themselves to your shape when you sit down, and
thick massago-rugs that rub your feet while you
walk, and all kinds of beautiful polished things. A lot
of it isn't quite real. The glowing fish that swim in a
holoquarium. The 3Ds of female dancers that float
above a projection table, wiggling their arms and legs
and dancing to music I can't hear.

The stink is real, though. Real enough to make your eyes water.

"Try not to breathe through your nose," Ryter advises.

I can tell from his expression that he's not terribly surprised by what he sees or smells. I follow him to the center of the room, where we find a kind of huge round bed that seems to be the source of the horrible stink. Imagine a throne made of thick sleeping mats and you've got the idea.

"The poor wretch," Ryter says softly.

Lying on the bed-throne is a shriveled, starving creature soaked in his own filth. Most of his hair has fallen out and lies in a fuzzy pile around his head. His teeth are gone, and his eyes are milky blind. I can barely make out the faded red monkey tattoo on his withered chest. At first glance you might think he's dead, but he isn't — not quite. His fingers twitch a little, and his mouth works, as if he's trying to speak, and you can see where veins pulse weakly in his scrawny neck.

A faint sound comes from his ruined mouth. "Mmm-mmm-mmm," like the noise of a small motor running out of power.

Amber lights slowly blink on the silver boxes of the mindprobe machinery, going, bzzzt bzzzt bzzzt. I get the idea the thing in the bed is trying to talk to the probe machine, or thinks the probe is talking to him. Something like that. The weird thing is, the filthy, bone-starved creature seems to be smiling, as if unaware of his condition.

"What happened to him?" I ask.

The young tek boss has worked up the courage to follow us into the room. "Mongo has been looping for more than a year," he says.

"Looping?" Ryter asks.

"A probe that keeps repeating in endless variations," the tek boss explains. "You never have to come out, if you don't want. This one is called *Forever Eden*, and it's his favorite trendie. Mongo is in Eden now, living the life of a proov. He refuses to leave. He loves it there."

A thick, grayish liquid oozes from around the needle stuck into the center of Mongo's naked skull. They call it brain ooze, and it happens when you probe for too long. They say that some of the more expensive probes last for twenty-four hours, but I never heard of anybody staying under for a whole year.

"So he's living in another world," Ryter says. "Or he thinks he is."

"Exactly," the tek boss says.

"Can we shut off the machine?"

"If we shut it off, he dies. It's the only thing

keeping him alive. The brain stimulation keeps his heart beating."

"I see," Ryter says. "And the reason nobody takes care of him or keeps him clean is because they're all terrified of Mongo the Magnificent?"

"Oh yes," the tek boss says. "There was a time when to enter this room without permission meant instant cancellation. Mongo killed many, often for no reason. To look directly into his eyes was a death sentence."

Ryter studies the tek boss. "Look around," he suggests. "Are you still frightened of Mongo?"

The tek boss slowly shakes his head.

"Somebody has to take charge of the latch," Ryter tells him gently. "Why not you?"

"Me?" the tek boss says, sounding terrified.

"You had courage enough to bring us here," Ryter says. "If someone doesn't take over, and soon, then all will be lost. Without guidance, without a leader to lead them, the Monkey Boys have degenerated. They'll tear you and your men apart and then destroy themselves."

"But why would they listen to me? I'm not a latch-boss."

"Neither was Mongo," Ryter points out, "until he made himself one."

•   •   •

After we leave, the young tek boss seals the hatch, but the stink of what happened to Mongo sticks with me. I'm thinking it could happen to Billy Bizmo, too, if he isn't careful. Part of me wants Billy to end up that way, for being so cruel about Bean, and the other part of me knows that as bad as the Bangers are, they'd be that much worse without someone to make the rules.

"What's your name, may I ask?" Ryter says to the tek boss.

"Gorm."

"That'll work," Ryter says, musing to himself. "The Great Gorm. Why not?"

Meanwhile the Great Gorm looks like he's going to be sick. The color has drained from his cheeks, he's breathing sort of puffy, and his eyes have this faraway focus, as if he's looking at tomorrow and doesn't much like what he sees.

"What if I fail?" he asks.

"You must banish all doubt," Ryter instructs him. "The other thing you must do is make up a few simple rules. That's what the Monkey Boys expect from their leader. A few rules strictly enforced."

Gorm thinks it over. You can tell he's slowly getting used to the idea of taking over from Mongo, and the more he thinks about it, the more he likes it.

"If I'm the boss, they'll have to obey me," he

mutters to himself. "Obey or die, that's the first rule."

Ryter nods, as if that's what he expected to hear. "I have a request for the Great Gorm," he says, bowing his head.

"What?" says Gorm, lost in his thoughts. "Oh yeah, sure. Go ahead."

"Two requests, actually. The first is that you release all prisoners as a gesture of goodwill," Ryter suggests. "My second request is that you banish us from the latch. Have a squad of teks escort us to the border."

Gorm looks at him sharply. "What? I assumed you'd stay and be my adviser."

"We have a mission elsewhere," Ryter says, making it sound grand and important. "But I do have one more piece of advice. Do not appoint an adviser until you're certain of your men. If I'm not mistaken, Mongo was adviser to the previous latchboss. The very one he assassinated."

Gorm glances nervously behind him, then catches himself. I notice he's already looking bigger and stronger. "Mongo made his proclamations from the East Tower," he says, eyes suddenly flashing. "The Great Gorm will do the same. I must tell them there's a new boss, new rules."

Ryter studies him thoughtfully and then nods. "The king is dead," he says. "Long live the king."

CHAPTER THIRTEEN

Miles to Go Before We Sleep

LITTLE FACE LOOKS scared. You can't blame him. The teks who drive us away in their takvee aren't exactly friendly. Plus a wild mob of Monkey Boys chase after the takvee, hooting and screeching and throwing stones at us. Every time a stone hits the armor plating, Little Face tries to make himself even smaller than he is. Also, he hasn't said "chox" since we left the fort.

"We'll be okay," I say, "soon as we're clear of this latch."

That's what I tell him, but inside I'm not so sure. Replacing the latchboss was a good idea, but it's not like he's actually taken control. It'll be a while before the Monkey Boys get used to the idea.

"How did you know about Mongo?" I ask Ryter.

He shrugs. "An educated guess. From the evidence

I assumed he was no longer in charge. I didn't know until we actually saw him."

Which kind of amazes me, because he seemed so sure at the time. I'm also thinking how different he's turned out, nothing like the pathetic old gummy who was willing to let me rob him rather than fight back. Except, of course, that I didn't end up stealing the only thing he really cares about. So I guess he was bluffing me, too, and I fell for it, just like the tek boss.

The takvee we're riding in is dark and cool inside, with soft black upholstery programmed to mold itself around you. Everything is padded and reinforced and armored. What looks like windows are really vidscreen images of the outside, because even armored windows can be broken, with the right weapon. If you listen you can hear the faint hum of the cyber-brain that monitors the weapon systems, and stays wide-eyed for danger. They say a really good tactical urban vehicle can think for itself, almost, protecting the riders.

I'm thinking it must be cool to be a latchboss, always cruising around in a new takvee, with all those teks ready to die for me, and then I flash on the thing on the bed-throne. Until I saw what happened to Mongo, I thought that getting canceled was the worst thing that could happen. Wrong. Being dead and not knowing it is much, much worse.

We pass into the shadows of the tall steel bones of buildings high against the sky, and for a while it's as dark as night. There could be things in the shadows. Lurking, almost invisible things that want us dead, but I can't be sure. For some reason that makes me think of Bean. Is that how the blood sickness makes her feel, like something is waiting in the shadows to take her away? Is she angry that it's happening to her and not someone else? Is she afraid? What?

I can't stand to think about it or I'll start screaming, so I concentrate on joking around with Little Face so he won't be scared.

"When we get where we're going, there'll be plenty of choxbars," I tell him. "Choxbars stacked as high as those old buildings over there. Do you believe me? Huh?"

I have to prod him, but Little Face finally bobs his head and almost smiles, and a few minutes later we're back at the Pipe. The teks more or less dump us out of the takvee and take off before we can even thank them. They're worried about the mob of wild Monkey Boys catching up, and so are we.

"I was hoping for stairs," Ryter says, looking at where the Pipe looms above us. "Or at least a ladder of some kind."

We have to make do with climbing the rubble

around the pylon. Little Face seems to be his old self now that our escape is in sight. He finds a path and leads us up the chunks of rubble. Ryter and me are both panting by the time we make it to the top, but Little Face, he's not even winded. He waits until we're almost there, gives us a big grin, and then jumps inside the open end of the Pipe. He claps his hands and chirps out, "Chox!" to let us know everything is okay.

I never thought that stupid word would sound so good.

This may sound fried, but the Pipe feels like home. We know the place, and what to expect, more or less. Even the rats are familiar, and not the least bit scary, compared to what we're leaving behind. The rats keep scurrying ahead of us, until their red eyes fade into the dimness.

"Lead on," Ryter says to me with a grand gesture. "'We've miles to go before we sleep. And promises to keep.'" After a moment, to let that sink in, he says, "That's from a poem."

I'm too numbed to ask what a poem is, but as usual the old gummy seems to know what I'm thinking.

"The man who wrote the poem was called Robert Frost. He lived in the twentieth century," he says.

"All that's survived of his poetry is that one line. But even one line is a kind of literary immortality."

"Lit-er-ary im-mortality," I say, mimicking his know-it-all voice. "What's that?"

"It means part of you lives forever," he explains. "The part of you that writes down words."

"Yeah? And what if nobody cares about the words?"

"Someday they will," he insists, and you can tell he believes that more than anything.

I don't know about words that make you live forever, but he's right about one thing. We've got miles to go, slogging along through the Pipe. Being careful to avoid the rusty holes and the clunky stuff that snags our feet.

There are parts of the Pipe that echo so much we sound like an army, and other parts where we can't hear anything, not even the skittery rats. Ryter says that's because of something he calls "acoostiks," but I think the Pipe has moods like a living thing. Noisy moods, quiet moods, dark moods. Sometimes it feels real peaceful and soothing, like the Pipe wants us to feel safe. Other times I'm so scared it feels like my knees are coming unscrewed or something. But it doesn't matter what we feel. The Pipe doesn't care. The Pipe keeps us moving.

I keep expecting Ryter to stop and rest because he's old and worn out, but he just plods along, never complaining, and after a while I get this idea that inside he's a lot stronger than he looks on the outside. Sometimes he's as quiet as the Pipe; other times he runs off at the mouth about books and words and other stuff nobody cares about anymore.

This one time he goes, "What's in a name, Spaz? You of all people should know."

"A name is just a word," I tell him. "It doesn't matter."

"No? What about Odysseus?"

"Who's Oh-dis-he-us?"

"Odysseus is many things. A name. A myth. A word."

"Yeah," I go, "a word nobody knows."

"A word I know. And if you listen, you'll know, too."

"Okay," I say. "Have it your way. I'm listening."

Ryter grunts in satisfaction. "In the beginning, Odysseus was just a man like any man. But he went on a long, dangerous journey, much as we are doing, and people spoke of it for generations, until eventually he became a myth. Later his adventures were written down in a book, and his name became the word for 'long, adventurous journey.' Odyssey."

"That's a stupid name," I say.

"Oh? Some would say that 'Spaz' is a stupid name."

That pulls me up short. I'm trying to see what his face says, but it's too dark. "Are you trying to bork me off?" I ask him, shoving my finger into his scrawny chest.

"No," he says gently. "I'm trying to make you think."

"I don't want to think!" I tell him. Actually, I'm shouting. "I just want to keep walking until we get there, okay? So forget about words and myths and all that gummy stuff you like to spew, and just keep walking!"

After that, it's quiet for a long time.

CHAPTER FOURTEEN

Fair Maidens
Must Be Rescued

WHEN WE FINALLY get to where the Pipe ends, the world is on fire.

I can smell it from miles away. At first the scent of the fire is just a tickle inside my nose, but after a while I can taste it on the back of my tongue. Kind of gritty and bitter and hot. The closer we get, the more we feel it in the air. The smoke makes Ryter cough, and when he coughs he seems really geezy and weak, and I'm worried he'll choke his withered old lungs out.

"I'm fine," he insists. "A little smoke can't stop us."

Going back isn't an option. If we go back we'll never find Bean, and besides, everybody we left behind wants to cancel us. So we keep going even though the Pipe is starting to feel hot under our feet.

We plod into the smoke for a long time. Nobody

speaks much — it's like the smoke has drained the talk right out of us. I'm getting worried we won't make it, when Ryter coughs out, "We're almost there."

The last section of the Pipe has come loose from the concrete pylons and it sags down, heading for ground level. The angle is so steep it's all we can do not to slip and fall, but there's one good thing: The smoke is a little thinner the lower we get.

It turns out the ragged, open end of the Pipe has sunk partway into the ground. We have to duck and crawl for the last few yards to get free of it.

The first thing we notice is the horizon on fire. It looks like the sun melted, and everything along the edge of the world went up in flames.

"Look at that," Ryter says, wheezing in amazement. "They're burning the whole latch."

The smoke brings us horrible smells. The kind of stink that makes you more afraid of the people who set it than the fire itself. My stomach is flip-flopping, and not just because I haven't eaten in a while. Everything's on fire in this place: buildings, stack-boxes, street hovels, people, even the dirt on the ground, all of it burning.

The scared part of me wants to run back into the Pipe and hide until things get better, but my brain knows things aren't going to get better anytime soon, if ever. We're stuck, and if we're not careful, we'll go up in smoke, too.

Ryter gathers me and Little Face close to him. "Our only chance is to stick together," he says.

The smoke is too thick to see very far, but we can hear the howling of the mob. The same kind of animal sound the Monkey Boys made, only worse. Even less human, like whatever happened in Mongo's old latch happened here, too, only it's been going on longer.

Then a different sound comes through the howling. A girl shouts, "Keep your distance! I warn you! Leave me alone or suffer the consequences!"

The girl's voice sounds frightened but strong, somehow, like she doesn't really believe anybody would dare hurt her, not even a mindless mob.

The smoke clears and we see her. A slender, beautiful girl standing on top of a broken-down takvee. She's not wearing body armor, just a flimsy, shimmering white gown and a silver headband. Howling attackers swarm around the takvee. They've snatched up packages of edibles, stuffing their dirty faces with food. Some of them are waving torches, reaching out their hands to grab her ankles.

"I am Lanaya, child of Eden!" she shouts. "Touch me and you'll die!"

It's the proov girl, the one from the Maximall, the

one who asked my name. Billy Bizmo said if I ever saw her again I should run for my life, because contact between proovs and normals is forbidden. But if me and Ryter don't do something, she's going to be set afire or torn to pieces, or both.

"You're sure she's the one?" Ryter asks when I tell him.

"I'm sure."

"Doesn't really matter who she is," he says, his eyes lighting up. "Fair maidens must be rescued."

"What can we do?"

Ryter thinks about it, his bleary old eyes flicking from the crazy mob swarming the takvee to the thick clouds of smoke that flow from the burning buildings.

"Wait here until you hear my signal. Then do your best."

"What?" I say. "What are you talking about?"

But Ryter has vanished into the smoke. I grab Little Face's hand before he disappears, too. "Crazy old man," I tell him. "What's he thinking?"

A moment later there's shouting from inside the smoke. "Edibles! Get him, he's got edibles!"

The mob hears that and they forget all about snatching the proov girl. Howling and waving their torches, they race off into the smoke, smelling blood, following the sound of the chase. Their eyes look al-

most blind, like all they can see is what they want —
in this case, edibles, food, something to eat.

Me and Little Face run up to the takvee. The proov
girl is staring into the smoke as if she can't believe
the mob has let her go.

"Quick," I tell her. "We've got to get out of here."

"You're the strange boy!" she exclaims, recogniz-
ing me. "The one called Spaz."

"Hurry," I say, offering my hand. "They'll be
back."

The proov girl takes my hand and jumps down.
"Why did they run away?" she asks.

"I'll explain later," I tell her. "How bad is your
takvee? Will it still run?"

"I don't know," she says. "They came out of
nowhere and surrounded us. When they saw we
couldn't move, my teks ran away."

"Get inside," I urge her, my eyes searching the
smoke for signs of the returning mob.

"Don't order me about," she says stiffly, like she's
queen of the world. "Do you know who I am?"

"Yeah," I say. "You're a dead proov if you don't
shut up and get inside."

She gives me a look like I'm garbage, no different
from the starving mob, but she ducks inside the
takvee. Me and Little Face shove in beside her.

"Can you drive this thing?" I ask her.

"Close doors!" she says, and I'm looking around for the handle when the doors close on their own. Voice activated. Of course. Stands to reason a proov would have the latest model.

"Forward!" she orders, and the takvee starts to move.

The vidscreens show nothing but smoke and ruin. I'm glad to be back in a takvee, escaping from the howlers, but part of me feels sick about Ryter. He must have known what would happen when he shouted "Edibles!" to a starving mob. They're probably tearing him to pieces right now, while we make our getaway, just like he planned.

"What were you doing here?" I demand of the proov girl, convinced that whatever happened to Ryter is her fault.

"Passing out food units," she says with a sniff. "In case you didn't notice, those people are hungry."

"I noticed," I tell her. "Hungry enough to eat you."

"They wouldn't dare."

I'm about to ask if her genetic improvement included brains — how could she be so stupid? — when someone runs out of the smoke in front of us.

"Stop!" I shout, and the takvee stops so hard we get thrown forward before the restraints can tighten.

"What are you doing?" the proov girl demands. "How dare you command my vehicle!"

It's Ryter. His raggedy clothes are torn even more, and there's blood on his arms. He's waving at us and grinning like he's totally zoomed.

"How do you open the door?" I ask the girl.

"Why should I?" she shoots back, looking pleased with herself.

"Because that old man just saved your life," I tell her.

She opens her mouth to make a wise remark, changes her mind, and says, "Door open!"

The door retracts. I reach out, grab Ryter, and haul him inside. The starving mob boils out of the smoke behind him. "Go!" I shout. "Go! Go!"

A moment later we're traveling at top speed, bouncing over the ruined landscape, crashing through the remains of charred buildings until we find an open path. The proov girl settles behind the console and issues crisp orders to the takvee, making sure we escape intact.

Beside me Ryter chuckles to himself. He holds up his arms, showing us the bite marks. "They wanted to eat me," he explains, sounding astonished. "That's how hungry they are. Hungry enough to eat a scrawny old gummy!"

"So why are you laughing?" I ask him.

"Am I? I didn't realize. Relief, I suppose. I'm just glad to be alive."

I'm glad, too, but I can't think of how to say it, so I reach over and squeeze his wrinkled hand.

"Good," I mutter. "That's good."

With the helium-shocks engaged, the takvee can go two hundred miles an hour, which means we're airborne about half the time. The nav systems keep us from colliding with obstructions like buildings hidden in the smoke, or roving mobs zoomed enough to throw themselves at a high-speed armored vehicle. The proov girl stays at the command console, watching the screens and indicators, but the takvee drives itself, obeying her verbal command to take us to a "safe place."

Three minutes later the takvee slows down and comes to a stop. The vidscreens show a gray, barren landscape. No people, no buildings, no rubble, no fire, no smoke, no nothing.

"We'll be safe enough here for the moment," the proov girl announces as the takvee winds down to idle.

"What is this place?" Ryter asks.

"Normals know it as 'the Forbidden Zone.' We just call it 'the Zone,'" she says, standing up from the console.

"Ah," says Ryter with a nod. "Is it still mined?"

The proov girl gives him a funny look, like, "How

did he know?" and then nods. "Of course," she says. "The mines are Eden's first line of defense. This vehicle has the codes to disarm them. If not, we'd already be blown to particles."

"So we can't get out and walk around?" he asks with a faint smile.

"Not if you want to live," she says. She hesitates, looking so regal and beautiful and perfect it makes me hurt inside. The usual reaction to being in the presence of a proov. Reminding me how pathetic it is to be born normal. "By the way," she says to Ryter, "thank you for distracting the mob."

"You're very welcome," says Ryter graciously. "And thank you for saving our lives, too."

She gives him a sharp look, like he got it wrong. "Oh, they wouldn't have dared harm me," she tells him. "They may be filthy and ignorant and starving, but even so, they know better than to touch a proov."

Ryter's old eyes look like he's laughing inside, even though his voice sounds very serious. "Perhaps," he says. "In any case, we filthy, ignorant normals are grateful for your help. For that matter, we have another favor to beg."

She raises her perfect eyebrows. "Oh?" she says, sounding very cool.

"Lanaya — may I call you Lanaya?"

Her response is somewhere between a nod and a

shrug, as if she couldn't care less what a wrinkled old gummy calls her.

"Lanaya, my young friends and I are on a mission. We must fight our way to the next latch and locate a certain young girl before it's too late."

"Too late?" Lanaya asks. "What do you mean by 'too late'?"

My throat finally decides to work. I tell her how a runner brought the message about Bean. How she's sick in her blood and wants to see me before she dies. How we've been struggling to get to her.

As Lanaya listens, the ice in her eyes melts and for a moment she almost looks like a normal. "This girl is your sibling?" she asks.

"She's my friend," I say.

Lanaya nods. She thinks about it for a moment and then announces: "I shall take you there."

CHAPTER FIFTEEN

In
the Zone

IT'S A VERY STRANGE FEELING, riding through a minefield. Knowing that if some little glitch goes wrong and our vehicle doesn't give out the right signal we'll be blown into particles, like Lanaya says. Not that it seems to bother her. She knows exactly where we are and where we're going, and has no doubt we'll get there in one piece.

"Eden is the center of the Urb," she explains, tapping her nav screen. "The Zone surrounds Eden on all sides. So we can get to any latch by circling through the minefields. No problem."

"No problem?" I ask, doubting her.

"I do it all the time," she says huffily. "Don't you know anything?"

The way she talks to me I should be mad, but for some reason I'm not. There's something about being a normal that makes you feel like you deserve it

when a proov looks down on you, because they're doing you a big favor just looking at you, period. So I
shut up and listen to Lanaya because I love to hear
her voice, even when she's telling me I'm stupid.
Also, she's so beautiful it hurts to look at her, but the
hurt feels good, which doesn't make any sense but I
swear it's true.

Proovs. Billy Bizmo is right: They're nothing but
trouble even if they *are* perfect.

"Lanaya," says Ryter, sounding very formal. "May
I ask what your guardians think of your excursions
into the Urb?"

"That's my business," she tells him. "I don't have
to justify myself to a normal."

Ryter seems amused by her response. "No, of
course you don't," he says. "Because you believe that
we normals are a much lower form of life than those
who have been genetically perfected. But I notice
that you seek out contact with us. Why is that? Just
for the thrill? The sense of danger? Or is there something more?"

Lanaya scowls, which only makes her even more
beautiful. "I don't have to help you people, you know."

"I know," Ryter says. "But you will."

"Oh, really?" Lanaya says scornfully. "How can
you be so sure? What do you know about me?"

"I know that in your heart you are brave and

good," he says. "And that's not a result of genetic improvement. You can't engineer goodness like you can engineer a perfect nose."

"What's wrong with my nose?" Lanaya exclaims, touching it.

"Absolutely nothing," Ryter tells her, sounding amused.

"You're an ignorant old man!" she says heatedly. "You have no right to speak of such things!"

"No right to say you're brave and good and have a perfect nose?" Ryter chuckles and rubs at his scraggly white beard. "Wait, I understand. What you really mean is, a normal doesn't have the right to speak on equal terms with a child of Eden. Yes, that's it," he adds, musing to himself. "You can't help but think that way. Superiority has been bred into you from the top of your head to the tips of your toes, and into every chromosome between. And yet still you come to the latches, first to experience adventure, and then to help. Which proves my initial impression, that you have a good heart, despite your breeding."

All Lanaya can manage to say is, "Hmmpf!" and then she turns away and busies herself with the console. Like she doesn't care what the old gummy thinks of her. Except even a dumb normal like me can tell she does care.

Ever since we made our escape, Little Face has

been staring at her like he's looking into the sun. When she turns her attention back to the command console, he crawls out of his seat and edges closer to her, like he's afraid he'll get burned but still he's willing to take the chance just to be near her.

"Chox?" he asks in his smallest voice.

Without really looking at him, Lanaya asks, "Is this child hungry?"

"He's always hungry," I tell her.

"Tell him I have no choxbars. They were taken by the mob."

"Tell him yourself," I say.

"How dare you be so impertinent!" she says.

"I'm not being impertinent," I explain, as gently as possible. "It's just that Little Face wants you to pay attention to him. That's why he asked for a choxbar. It's the only way he knows how to talk."

Lanaya swivels her beautiful head at me. "You mean 'chox' is the only word he knows?" When I nod, she says, "We'll see about that!" Then she smiles at Little Face and goes, "My name is Lanaya. Can you say 'Lanaya'?"

Little Face crawls back to his seat, where he snuggles up next to me, hiding his eyes from the beautiful proov girl.

"What did I do?" Lanaya asks, sounding upset.

"You did nothing wrong," Ryter assures her. "He's

a feral child. No mother, no father, no one to care for him or raise him or teach him how to be human. So he's existed much like an animal, without language. He thinks in images, not words."

"How strange," says Lanaya, sounding amazed.

Ryter shakes his head sadly. "Not strange, I'm afraid. His condition is all too common in the latches. And becoming more common every day."

Suddenly an electronic voice speaks from the console. "PATROL VEHICLE APPROACHING," it announces.

"Uh-oh," Lanaya says. She issues a command to the takvee: "Evasive action. Keep out of range."

The takvee turns and picks up speed.

"What's wrong?" I ask.

"Eden security patrol," she explains. "We're not supposed to be here. No one is. That's why they call it the Forbidden Zone."

"Right," I say, feeling dumber than ever.

"If they catch us, will we be detained?" Ryter asks.

"They wouldn't dare," Lanaya tells him. "But I'd be reported."

She makes being reported sound worse than being detained, but the way it works out, the takvee avoids the security patrol no problem and before long we're crossing out of the Zone into the next latch.

The latch where Bean lives. If she still lives, which is something I can't stand to think about, so I don't. Of course she still lives, she has to. Bean wouldn't dare not be alive when we've taken all this trouble to get to her, would she?

"Something wrong?" Ryter asks me.

"No," I tell him. "I'm fine."

"Uh-oh," Lanaya says again. But this time it's not the Eden security patrol she's worried about. It's what has come out of the rubble to greet us. Vandals swarming from nowhere on their jetbikes, waving splat guns and forcing us to stop.

And there, riding high and mighty on the biggest jetbike, is someone I know, someone I hoped never to see again.

Lotti Getts, boss of the Vandals, boss of the latch.

CHAPTER SIXTEEN

In the Latch
of the Vandal Queen

BOSS LADY. The Latch Queen. Nails. The White Widow.

Lotti has a lot of names, none of them good. Nails because she has special razors glued onto her long fingernails, razors that'll spill your red so quick and deep, you won't even feel it. White Widow because most of her luvmates don't seem to live very long. She has other names, too, names that are only whispers, names that'll get you canceled if she hears.

The first and only time Lotti Getts ever noticed me was the day I lost my family unit. And on that day Lotti tickled me with her razor nails, looked at me with eyes of stone, and said, "You've got bad blood, boy, and we can't have that in our latch, can we?"

Now we're surrounded by her gang the moment

we cross into her territory. Like they knew we were coming.

"Nothing to worry about," Lanaya announces, sounding almost cheerful. "They know me here."

Before I can say anything, she pops out the top hatch and waves a greeting. "I come to trade!" Lanaya announces. "Let me pass!"

The Vandals rev their jetbikes so loud it makes the air feel as thick as jelly. So loud you can almost see the noise shimmering. Exhaust flames scorch the ground, and the Vandals are all grinning in that hard, mean way they have, like they can't wait to hurt something.

Lotti Getts raises her fist. When the engines fade away she stands up in her saddle and stares hard at Lanaya. Most normals would be afraid to stare like that at a proov, but not Lotti.

"What trade have you?" Lotti demands.

Me and Ryter and Little Face are hiding in the takvee and watching on the vidscreens, but even so I can tell that Lanaya is surprised by the question. Like nobody ever dared ask her before. "The, um, usual items," she says, sounding uncertain. "Is there a problem?"

"Yes, there's a problem," Lotti says. "Someone has been running mindprobes into my latch. Probing is forbidden here, under penalty of death." The jetbikes rev, as if in agreement.

"I'm not a runner," Lanaya protests. "I don't know anything about mindprobes."

"No?"

Lotti gets off her jetbike, climbs up on the hood of the takvee like she's mounting a throne in her stab-heel boots, and stands eye-to-eye with Lanaya. All around there's maybe five hundred of her best and meanest Vandals armed to the teeth with splat guns and gut-rippers and armor-piercing crossbows. If Lotti gives the signal, they'll fight until they win, or die. That's the rule of the Vandals, win or die. And they always win.

"What are you hiding?" Lotti demands.

"Hiding?" says Lanaya. "Nothing."

"We'll see about that," says Lotti. And with one hand she lifts Lanaya right out of the hatch and sets her down on the hood. On the vidscreen Lanaya's face looks astonished, like her whole world just got tilted.

The next thing we know Lotti is looking down into the open hatch. She doesn't seem a bit surprised to find us there. "Two choices," she says, smiling with her teeth. "Come out or I'll firebomb this vehi-cle with you in it."

We come out. Ryter first, then Little Face, then me.

"I can explain, my lady," says Ryter, in his grandest voice.

"Don't 'lady' me," Lotti snarls. "And don't explain. I see what I see," she says, looking hard at me. "And what I see is a traitor, a rule breaker, a latch runner."

"Don't hurt them," I say. "They were just trying to help me."

Lotti seems delighted to hear it. "Helping you disobey your latchboss is a killing offense," she says. "You knew that?"

I nod.

"We all knew it," Ryter says.

"Shut your hole, geez! I'm talking to the spaz boy. Tell me, Spaz boy, what's in my latch worth risking your life for?"

My heart is pounding so fierce, I can hardly think, but I know if I don't tell Lotti, she'll slice the truth out of me anyway. "My sister," I tell her. "I want to see my sister."

I get the idea Lotti already knows why I'm here, that she heard all about it from Billy Bizmo. They say Billy was once her luvmate, one of the few who survived, and that's why whenever there's a latch war, Lotti and Billy are usually on the same side.

Lotti gets in my face, so close I can smell the anger on her breath. Like the air after lightning strikes.

"Give me a reason," she says. "A reason to let you live."

"Let me see Bean and I'll do anything you want."

She strokes her razor nails under my chin. "That's not a reason," she says.

"I'm begging you."

"There's a rule against begging, Spaz boy."

I decide maybe it's better to shut up. Lotti's just playing with us. She doesn't really care why we're here, or what we want. "You'll do anything, eh?" she says, turning the idea around in her mind. "Hmmm, that might be interesting. Let me confer with my warriors."

The way Lotti saunters back to the Vandals, you know she rules the ground she walks on. We can't hear what her gang brutes have to say, but several of them nod and glance at us as they talk among themselves.

A few moments later she comes back to the takvee. "I, Lotti Getts, queen of the Vandals, boss of the latch, task you with this. Find me the probe runner. Deliver the vermin into my hands, and Spaz may visit his wretched sister. That is my ruling."

Ryter strokes his wispy beard and says, "But my lady, there may not be time. We must —"

"Shut it!" Lotti shrieks. "Do as I command, old man. Bring me the probe runner! Do it or die!"

Even if we'd dared to object, we couldn't have made ourselves heard over the air-shaking rumble of the jetbikes, or the earsplitting cheer of the Vandals chanting for their queen.

"Nails! Nails! Nails!" they roar. "Nails! Nails! Nails!"

Finally she rakes the cool gray sky with her red-cutting fingernails and fixes me with a pay-attention stare that says without speaking: *I mean it, boy, find me the probe runner or die trying.*

CHAPTER SEVENTEEN

Looking for Probes in All the Wrong Places

THE FIRST THING Lanaya wants to know is, can we get away with disobeying. "I mean, what's to stop us from finding your sister and then just running away?" she asks.

Ryter sighs and looks at me, like he thinks I'm the one who should tell her.

"Lotti will have my family unit under watch," I explain. "Just by coming here I've put them all in danger. We don't have any choice. We have to find this stupid probe runner."

Some runners carry messages, but some carry things to trade, forbidden things, and Lotti has forbidden probing in her territory. She must have seen what happened in the nearby latches when gangs spent more time probing than taking care of business.

"She's an intelligent leader," Ryter offers. "Brutal

but brilliant. If Mongo had been half as smart, he'd still be Mongo the Magnificent."

We're back in the takvee, trying to put some distance between us and the Vandals. I expected them to follow, but so far they haven't. Maybe Lotti thinks we'll have a better chance of finding the runner if she's not around. The trouble is, I've no idea where to start. I feel like I'm slowly falling down a bottomless black hole and the more I try to get out, the deeper I go. The worst part is, I'm dragging everybody else down with me.

"We must think deeply," Ryter suggests. "All of us. Put our heads together and come up with a plan."

The takvee rolls to a stop in a deserted area known to locals (and I used to be a local, remember) as the Brick Yard. All that's left of the old buildings are huge piles of broken bricks slowly eroding into dust. Nothing lives here anymore. Nothing on two legs, that is. Even on the vidscreens the red eyes of long-tailed rodents wink like stars among the brick mountains. On certain nights — the blackest nights — the Brick Yard comes alive with a chittering that sounds like conversation, as if all the rats are trying to talk at once.

I don't mention the rats, but Ryter notices me shivering.

"We'll think of something," he promises. "Lanaya,

my dear, do you have any thoughts? If you were on your own, how would you go about identifying a probe runner?"

Lanaya shrugs. "I don't know. Find where to buy the probes, I guess. That's where I'd start."

"Excellent!" Ryter exclaims. When the old man gets excited, his face looks younger, as if ideas have the power to melt the years away. "It has the advantage of simplicity," he says, rubbing his withered hands together, "and the best ideas begin with simplicity. Yes indeed, child, I believe you've struck on a viable strategy. If we find a source for the forbidden mindfliks, we may be able to make a connection to the person supplying them — namely the probe runner."

An idea blinks into my head. "What if we pretend we want to trade for probes?" I ask.

"Yes!" Ryter says. "Yes! Yes! Make him come to us! Brilliant!"

And that's how we hatch a plan to become criminals, and enter the very dangerous underworld of traders who deal in things forbidden in the latch of the Vandal Queen.

Lanaya takes us to Traderville, where hundreds of merchants keep their stalls, and even the strolling beggars have things to trade. She's been there before and knows where to leave the takvee, and who to see.

"Let me do the talking," she announces. "They know me here," she adds, with her beautiful nose up in the air. Making sure that we never forget she's Little Miss Genetically Perfect.

Traderville is this crowded-up jumble of stalls and shacks and security shelters shoved together under the old skyrails. They say in the backtimes that trains flew through the air, just overhead. Trains that moved so fast, they made their own wind. Trains that went faster than the sound they left behind. It might even be true, but the trains are gone now, and all that remains is the old elevated track system. Parts of it fall from the sky now and then, but that doesn't stop the merchants from gathering there to trade and haggle — and steal, if they can.

They say "trader" is just another word for "thief." I don't know if that's true, exactly, but you have to be very careful or you'll go into a stall to trade for clothes, let's say, and end up without a shirt on your back. I know because it happened to me once. Charly, my former dad, told me I'd learned a valuable lesson that was worth more than the stupid old shirt. As far as I'm concerned, the valuable lesson was "don't bother complaining to Charly." And, like they say, don't give up your goods until the trade is on the table.

Lanaya leads us to the most densely crowded part of Traderville, under the rusty metal awnings that provide shade from the naked sun, or protection from the acid rain, depending on the weather. The stalls display goods from all over the Urb. Boots from Latch West, velvet capes made by the famous Beastie slave girls, ironware for cooking, every kind of edible, weaponry, body armor, exotic luv-scents guaranteed to "cloud men's minds," herbs and potions and poisons, holos and 3Ds, cheap crib gear (inflato chairs that leak), expensive crib gear (inflatos that don't leak), thumpers and flutes, three-legged dogs (It Barks And It Bites But It Can't Run Away!), twenty-eight flavors of noodle, and last but not least, choxbars.

First thing, Lanaya trades her earrings for a new stock of edibles. She hands Little Face a choxbar, and almost before he gets the wrapper off he's grinning like he's just been made king of the latch. "Chox!" he chirps, clinging to her shimmering white gown. "Lan-ay-ah chox!"

That freezes me. I save the brat's life more than once, and let him come along with us, but he learns to say her name, not mine? Lanaya gives me a look that says, *see, I told you,* but I pretend not to be annoyed. We've got more important things to worry about.

"This way," Lanaya says. "I know exactly the man to see."

She leads us to one of the larger stalls, where three lovely young women offer a variety of luv-scents. They make their pitch to Ryter, holding out their scented bottles and chanting, "Essence of orchid! Essence of rose! Come on, old man, put it under your nose!" as if they assume he wants to buy luv-scents for the beautiful young proov girl.

Ryter waves them off with a smile while Lanaya gets right down to business. "I must speak with your master," she says, keeping her voice low. "Is Bender here?"

"Bender is always here," trills one of the luv-scent girls. She makes a funny, birdlike noise, somewhere between a whistle and a laugh, and the man himself appears from behind the curtains at the back of the stall.

When he sees who has summoned him, Bender's face lights up. "My dear!" he exclaims. "What a wonderful surprise!"

They say "fat as a rich man" because only the rich can afford enough edibles to make them fat. If it's true, then Bender must be very rich indeed. He wears the proof of his wealth like some men wear body armor, and he keeps patting his wonderfully plump belly as if to make sure he's well-protected by his layer of hard-earned blubber. His face is as round as the rest of him, and just as jolly. Everything about Bender looks jolly except his eyes, which are small and bright and watchful. As he carefully looks us over, he fingers the many small gold rings that are woven into his silky black beard.

"I see you have taken a new escort, my dear. Did your teks displease you somehow?"

"Indeed they did," Lanaya says, offering no further explanation. She beckons to Bender, drawing him closer, which seems to make him more than a little nervous. "I'm interested in trading for probes, Bender," she whispers huskily. "Can you help me?"

Bender shrinks away as if she's cut him. "Oh no, my dear! Probing is forbidden in this latch! Merely to possess a probe means instant cancellation. To actually trade for them means even worse."

"Worse than death?" Lanaya asks curiously.

"Oh indeed, there are many things worse than death, and the Latch Queen knows them all. Forget about probing, I beg you."

"But surely a proov isn't bound by the same rules," Lanaya says, coaxing him. "Surely an exception can be made for me?"

She reaches out as if to stroke the rings woven into Bender's beard, but he hastily pulls away. "No, my dear, not possible!"

"But you've made many such exceptions in the past."

The trader shakes his head so hard that the rings in his beard chime and all of his many chins wobble. "Not for probes, my dear. Never for probes. Anything else I'll happily trade, but not that. Gold, silver, gemstones, these I can provide. But not the other." Bender has been slowly backing up, trying to put distance between himself and the dangerous proov girl, but she won't let him get away. Lanaya finally hooks her fingers into his beard rings and draws him close. She whispers something in his ear, he nods fearfully, then whispers something back.

Lanaya returns to us with a secret smile. "Come along," she says, looking very pleased with herself. "It's not far from here."

She leads us behind the stalls, into the darkest part of Traderville. To the place where armored thugs guard each shack, and luv-girls beckon from the open windows. You can buy anything in this place, from dice-bones to a human life. My first impulse is to cover Little Face's eyes, but I know he's seen worse, like every child on the curb.

Lanaya doesn't seem to notice all the wickedness

and filth. As if somehow it isn't real to her. Which makes me think that nothing in the world of normals is quite real to her. Maybe that's why she acts as if nothing can touch her, because she thinks we're all part of an exciting, entertaining game called Proov Princess Visits the Latch.

Ryter glances at me and shakes his head. He looks worried, if not for himself then for the rest of us. It's not unusual for people to enter this part of Traderville and never be seen again. I'm about to say something, when Lanaya holds up her hand.

"Be still," she commands. "We must wait here while the Furies check us out."

Furies, I'm thinking, what Furies?

And then I see them. Figures in black-hooded capes, creeping out from between the shacks. It's not until they're close enough to touch that I notice the skull masks and the black daggers, and by then it's too late.

CHAPTER EIGHTEEN

Mark of
the Assassin

IT'S AMAZING HOW Furies can blend into the shadows without making a sound. Their skull masks are the mark of the assassin — that and the black daggers. I've heard about Furies, of course, but never seen one. Supposedly they have to be female. Not that you can tell the female part; it could be anybody or anything inside the hooded black capes.

They say Furies are so cunning and stealthy, their victims die without uttering a sound. All I can do is hold tight to Little Face and hope that Lanaya knows what she's doing.

"Greetings," she says quietly, as the Furies move silently around her. "We bring offerings to Vida Bleek."

My heart clenches when she speaks that name. Vida Bleek is boss of the underworld traders and in his own way as powerful as the Latch Queen. He deals in all things stolen or forbidden, and nobody gets the best of him and lives to brag about it. I can tell Ryter has heard of Bleek, too, because his eyes are as big as targa stones. We look at each other but we don't dare speak, afraid that the wrong word will trigger the Furies.

Lanaya has no such fear. "I'm a child of Eden," she says, ignoring the daggers that dance beneath her elegant nose. "Tell Bleek I must see him on a matter of great urgency."

Notice she doesn't say "please," not even to dagger-waving assassins. My brain tells me the proov girl is maddeningly stupid to taunt the Furies, but my heart thinks she's also incredibly brave, braver than I'll ever be.

"Quickly!" Lanaya demands. "We haven't got all day!"

That's it, I'm thinking, and I'm hoping the daggers are sharp and true so we won't suffer much. And then before I can let out the breath I've been holding, the Furies seem to vanish and a small, hairless figure emerges from the darkness.

"Offerings?" the small man asks. "Did I hear the word 'offerings'? What have you brought me, besides your lives?"

Vida Bleek stands with his tiny arms folded across his chest, looking up at Lanaya with an expression of curiosity. As if he's discovered a rare gemstone he'd just love to pluck from its setting. The only big thing about him is his eyes, which seem to blaze with intelligence and cunning. Lanaya is at least twice as tall as Bleek, but he doesn't seem to mind. How big you are doesn't matter when you have the Furies at your command.

"Whatever it takes," Lanaya tells him. "That's what I bring."

"You're rich," he says with a shrug. "But then all proovs are rich. What is it you want, exactly?"

Lanaya taps a finger against her forehead. "Probes," she says. "Mindprobes."

Bleek's teeth are small, too, when he smiles. There's nothing friendly about the smile, though. It's a smile that wants to chew you into little bits. You can almost hear his mind whirring as he tries to figure an advantage. Behind him the Furies blend themselves into the darkness, waiting for his command, as silent as eternity.

"Probing has been forbidden in this latch," he says, as if making idle conversation. "You must know that."

"Many things are forbidden," Lanaya says. "That just makes them more valuable."

"Not every forbidden thing carries a sentence of death," Bleek says, rubbing a hand over his hairless head. "Do you know what happened to the last mope who said 'probe' to me?"

"I'm not a mope," Lanaya reminds him. "I'm a child of Eden."

"Yeah," goes Bleek, sounding unimpressed. "But what makes you think proovs are invulnerable? If you cut a proov, does she not bleed? Hmmm? Tell you what, child of Eden. We'll have a sitdown. I'll do that much for you. Step into my office."

We follow him into a shack. The only light inside the shack is a single candle that barely pushes the shadows back. I figured a man as powerful as Vida Bleek would live in splendor, but everything is plain and unadorned. The walls are bare. The rug on the floor is worn thin. If Bleek has anything to trade — and he must — he doesn't keep it here. Then I realize this isn't really his "office," it's just a place of convenience, the nearest shack. He figures we're not worthy enough to need impressing.

Bleek settles himself on the rug and bids us to do the same. After we sit, several of the Furies glide in, hugging the walls. Once they've stopped moving they remain as still as hooded statues. I'm so scared of them, I don't even want to know what they look like under their skull masks.

"What have we here?" Bleek asks, indicating

me and Ryter and Little Face. "Is this your idea of an escort?"

"These are my friends," Lanaya says, and tells him our names.

"Spaz," Bleek says, looking directly at me. "I remember that name. You were banned from this latch, were you not? And now you return in the company of an old man, a boy, and a proov. Very strange. What is your explanation?"

I try to shrug as casually as possible, like traveling from latch to latch is no big deal. "I, um, wanted to visit my family unit," I tell him.

Bleek seems to find my explanation amusing. "Just drop in and say hello?"

"Something like that."

His small teeth shape themselves into a grin. "Feel free to lie, boy. I often find lies more interesting than the truth. They say more about the liar. And you, old man, what of you?"

Ryter spreads his hands. They tremble a little, but not as much as my own. "One last adventure," he says. "One last chance to see the world before the lights go out."

Bleek nods and then turns to Lanaya. "The most interesting lie remains yours," he tells her. "You pretend an interest in probes and yet I can see at a glance you've never experienced one. Therefore you want information about probing for some other purpose. Treachery, no doubt."

"No," says Lanaya.

"Silence!"

The room seems to shrink as the Furies draw closer.

Bleek's eyes blaze, as if he's been lit from within by the candle. The light is cruel and angry. "You proovs have a weakness — you assume that all normals are ignorant. Do you think a man keeps a position like mine by being stupid? Let me tell you something, my fine young proov: I trade in more than forbidden things. I trade in information. And my information tells me you're here to please the Latch Queen by betraying the probe runner. Do you deny this?" he asks quietly. "Hmm? Do you?"

Lanaya shakes her head.

"Good," he says, satisfied. "What you may not know is that for some reason the Latch Queen fears me. She thinks I want to get rid of her and take over the latch myself. She has a point. Why should I pay her tribute, eh? When she does nothing for me, hmm? When my Furies can strike without warning? Tell me, who is feared more, the brutish, noisy Vandals or my silent, cunning assassins. Hmm?" Bleek doesn't expect an answer. He's telling us his plans because he's so pleased with himself, and because he knows it makes us afraid. "Have I shocked you?" he asks. "Didn't know what you were getting into, did you?"

Lanaya takes a deep breath and says, "May we leave?"

Bleek laughs. It sounds like a series of little shrieks, eek-eek-eek, like he stores up all the pain he inflicts and uses it when he laughs. "Leave," he says, "but we're just becoming acquainted!"

"But we still have to find the probe runner," Lanaya insists.

Bleek shakes his small, deadly head. "You don't get it, do you? Let me ask you this: Who brings us the probes and the equipment to use them?"

"If I knew that —" Lanaya begins.

"You know nothing! Probes, probes! Who cares about probes? Not the Latch Queen. She doesn't really want to ban them; she just wants more tribute."

"But she said — "

"Silence!" the little man roars, his voice as sharp and cold and quick as a chetty blade. "Are you really that stupid, Proov? Don't you know that you and probes both come from the same place?"

"That's ridiculous," Lanaya says, flustered.

"No. All probes come from Eden."

"I don't believe it," says Lanaya.

"No?" says Bleek, who seems pleased by her

denial. "Look around. Do you think we possess the technology to develop mindflix? Or brain probes? Or the equipment to make them work? We who beg edibles from the likes of you? We who live in squalor and despair? We who risk our lives to jam needles into our brains so we can pretend to live in Eden until our minds burn out? Hmm? Hmm? Your ignorance is an insult! I don't care what that wretched Latch Queen says, you're too stupid to live."

Bleek makes a small sign with his left hand, and the Furies advance, daggers raised.

"Wait!" cries Ryter.

That's when the air begins to move. The candle flickers out. Something big is coming, something big enough to make its own wind. My heart beats once and then it washes over us, the earthshaking roar of jetbikes, the scream of attacking Vandals, the dull, ugly explosion of splat guns.

The Furies vanish in an instant, taking Bleek with them. The walls of the shack split open, and the noise of the jetbike engines is so loud I can't think. Ryter tries to scream something but I can't hear him. He grabs Little Face and runs through the opening in the walls. Lanaya tugs at me and, when I don't move, she slaps my face.

That does it. I'm awake now, and following Lanaya,

following her shimmering white gown. Around us the world explodes. I bounce off the side of a jetbike, see the silent, screaming face of a Vandal warrior. One of the Furies clings to his back, dagger poised. I don't know what happens next because I'm running into the night, away from the insane roar of the battle, running, running, running for my life.

CHAPTER NINETEEN

Spaz Boy Melts
in the Acid Rain

TRADERVILLE IS DESERTED. The busy stalls have been emptied and boarded up. All that remains are a few metal storage cans some trader must have dropped in his hurry to get away when the Vandals roared through.

A light rain falls from the dark sky and goes pip! pip! pip! on the hollow cans.

Pip! pip! pip!

I'm standing there like a googan with the rain running down the back of my neck. My insides feel as hollow as those stupid empty cans, like I'm going pip! pip! pip! inside because I was so scared. Too scared to move until the proov girl slapped me. Too scared to help anyone but myself. Too scared to do anything but run. Too scared, even, to think of Bean.

No, that's a lie. That's really why I feel so hollow and miserable. I did think of Bean, but I was wishing she'd never sent for me, wishing I'd never come. Blaming her because we'd got ourselves stuck in the middle of a turf battle between the Latch Queen and her rival. Like it's Bean's fault I'm a rotten coward.

So I'm standing out in the acid rain, letting the warm itch of it nibble at my skin, and thinking if it rains long enough I'll dissolve and my problems will be over. Spaz boy melts. Good riddance.

I'm thinking about opening my mouth and seeing if maybe I'll drown faster, when Ryter comes limping out of the rain. He's leaning on his walking stick pretty hard, holding himself up, and there's a lot of hurt in his ancient eyes. He gives me a tired old smile and says, "So, you made it. Good."

Good for what? I'm thinking. "You're hurt," I tell him.

"Just bruised," he says. "Nothing serious. One of those horrible jetbikes knocked me down. They'll be the death of me someday, I suppose. But not today."

"What about the others?"

"Lanaya and the boy have gone to get the takvee," he says. Then he looks at me, really looks at me, and goes, "What's wrong, son? Have you been wounded?"

I shake my head and look away.

"Ah," says Ryter knowingly. "You were scared and ran. So what? We all ran. There were too many of them and not enough of us. What else could we do?"

I shrug.

"This may work in our favor," Ryter says, trying to cheer me up. "It's obvious the Latch Queen was just using us to get at Vida Bleek and his assassins. Distract him with us while she attacks. I doubt she really cares about the menace of mindprobes. Or maybe she does, who knows? The point is, right now she's got her hands full. She'll need all of her people fighting by her side. So the way is clear."

I keep staring at the wet ground and go, "Huh?" like a major mope.

"Your family unit," says Ryter. "Your sister. The Latch Queen can't spare the men to guard them, not with a battle going on."

If I hadn't been feeling so lowdown I'd have thought of that myself. The old man is right. We're almost there, with nothing to stop us if we hurry. Suddenly I can't feel the rain. All I can feel is the need to see Bean. Be alive, I'm thinking, please be alive.

I stayed alive for you. Now you stay alive for me.

A takvee is amazingly quiet for a heavily armored vehicle. Lanaya glides it up behind us and the first thing we hear is her voice going, "Come on, quick!" and then, "Lan-ay-a Chox!" as Little Face chimes in. It turns out she's letting the kid pretend to drive the takvee. He's bouncing around at the console, giggling and making all sorts of explosive little kid noises. Probably stuff he picked up when the Vandals attacked, and now it's all part of his pretend game, which is just as well.

The proov girl asks me where my family unit lives, exactly. When I tell her, she programs the takvee and we get underway.

Ryter groans a little as he sits down, but waves off any offers to help. "Fortunes of war," he mutters. "War and old age. I'll be fine. Wake me when we get there," he adds, and then falls deeply asleep, just like that.

Sleep, after what we've been through? I don't know how he does it. My blood still feels electrified. Lanaya seems just as jumpy, as if she can barely stop herself from leaping out of the takvee and running on her own power.

I want to tell her how brave she is, how perfect, but something inside won't let me speak. Maybe because I don't want to remind her of how terrified I'd been when she'd slapped my face and saved my life.

"Did you notice?" she asks me, her beautiful eyes glowing with excitement. "Did you see what happened?"

I don't know what she's talking about and say so.

"They could have canceled us but they didn't,"

she whispers, so we don't wake Ryter. "The way those Furies fought, it was as if they were helping us get away. The Vandals, too. The only reason we're alive is because they wanted us to survive."

"Because you're a proov?"

"I don't know," she says, puzzled. "Maybe. But I think something else is going on. We were caught in the middle of a power struggle between the Latch Queen and an ambitious crime boss, right? We broke all the rules on both sides. But when they had a chance to cancel us, they didn't. And it wasn't just because I'm a proov."

"Then why?"

"I think it had something to do with you. The Latch Queen was expecting you. So was Vida Bleek. Excuse me, but why would they even be aware of some spastic nobody?"

" 'Nobody'?" I say as my face gets hot.

"That's my point, silly. *Because you're not a nobody.* You're important enough to attract the attention of all those powerful people: Billy Bizmo, Lotti Getts, Vida Bleek. Why is that?"

"I don't know," I tell her. "I never thought about it."

"Maybe you should," Lanaya says. "Think about it, I mean."

But there isn't room in my head right now for thinking about things I don't understand. There's only room for hoping that Bean will still be there, and that she isn't as bad off as the runner made it sound.

As we get closer I start to recognize more and more of the old neighborhood. The cellar holes where we played hide-or-cancel, the stalls where we traded for edibles, the alleys where we chose up teams and pretended to be Vandals fighting the invaders. There's nobody on the streets now, though. No enforcers, no kids going wild in the night, no frightened folk scuttling from door to door. They must be hunkered down inside their shelters, aware of the not-so-distant battle. Not knowing if Lotti Getts and her gang will remain in power, or if Vida Bleek and his Furies will take over the latch.

"We're almost there," I say.

Ryter wakes up. There's pain and worry in his bleary old eyes, but joy and triumph, too. He squeezes my shoulder. "Are you ready for this, son? It may not be easy."

My mouth feels like dry sand. "I know."

This is what I know: The only thing worse than finding Bean dead will be watching her die.

Get ready for worse, Spaz boy, my brain says. You of all people should know there's nothing so bad it can't get worse.

CHAPTER TWENTY

What Bean Believed

ONCE WHEN SHE WAS four years old, Bean decided she wanted to go to Eden. She didn't know it was a real place. She thought we could walk there with our eyes closed and just pretend. "Walk me to Eden," she asked me, "please please please?" So I took her hand and we walked out through the dark alley behind our building, and then farther, until I found a patch of sunshine among the ruins. "Do you feel that?" I said as the sun warmed our faces. "That's Eden shining on us." Bean kept her eyes closed the whole time because she didn't want to spoil it. She never told Charly or Kay because it was our secret.

The bad thing is, from then on Bean thought I could do just about anything. I'd taken her to Eden and so I could make it stop raining, or fix a boo-boo, or make Charly and Kay stop fighting. Or make her better when she got sick. "All you have to do is close your eyes," she'd say. "Make it happen, please?"

I wish I could close my eyes now. Then I wouldn't see the bullet marks above the door of my old family shelter, or the coils of cutwire blocking the entrance. The bullet marks and the cutwire have always been there, ever since I can remember, but they still make me sad.

At first nothing happens when I bang my fist on the door. Then an eye fills the peephole and Charly unlocks and opens up. "You," he says, sounding surprised. Not angry or disappointed, just surprised. A moment later Kay, my foster mom, she comes running in. As soon as she sees me, her eyes fill with tears. She doesn't hug me or anything. Kay was never much for hugs. Instead, she hugs her own arms and says, "Who are these people?"

She means Ryter and Little Face.

"These are my friends," I say, and introduce them. Little Face hides behind me, acting shy. Ryter gives a little bow, bending forward over his walking stick, and says, very formal, "Pleased to meet you, madam."

And then Lanaya comes out from behind the door and Charly almost falls down.

"Oh," he says. "Oh!"

I don't know if Charly has ever seen a proov up

close before, and it's like he doesn't want to see her now. Or he's afraid to look but can't help staring. Probably he doesn't know what to think, or how to act.

"I brought you some edibles," Lanaya says, holding out a small bag.

Kay takes the bag like it might explode.

"I've come to see Bean," I manage to say. "Where is she?"

"Our daughter is sick," Charly mutters. "Very sick."

"She's been asking for you," Kay says, so softly she can barely be heard. "I told her you couldn't come. I told her it was against the rules."

Nobody tries to stop me as I cross the outer room and find the entrance to Bean's cubicle. When I draw back the curtain my hands feel so light it's like they're not connected to my arms. At first I think she's not there, because the mat on the floor looks empty. Just a couple of scruffy old blankets. And then the blankets move and a skull-like face peeks out at me, with big eyes sunk in dark circles. There are lumps on her neck from swollen glands.

"Spaz!" Bean says, wheezing. "I knew you'd come! I knew it!"

Then I'm kneeling beside the mat and pressing my wet face against her face and I'm so glad she's alive, I don't care how bad she looks. She's still Bean inside, you can hear it in her voice. But when I draw back to look at her again, she's so thin and pale and wasted away it almost stops my heart. "Oh, Bean," I say. "I'm sorry."

"Don't be sorry," she says. "My dad said you couldn't come, but you know what? He sent for you anyhow."

So Charly had paid for the latch runner. I know he did it for Bean and not for me, but I don't care. I'm here, and that's all that matters.

Later, Kay tells me the healer stopped coming ten days ago. "There's nothing more she can do. No one can stop the blood sickness. Bean takes her remedy, but it doesn't help."

Ryter has settled his old bones on the floor and he looks so peaceful it makes me feel better. "The disease used to be called leukemia," he tells us, "and I think they had real cures for it, in the backtimes."

"What kind of cures?" I demand.

Ryter shakes his head. "Sorry, son. I've no idea. The knowledge was lost long ago."

"Then why'd you mention it? It's just backtimer bull, that's all it is," I say, feeling cranked enough to hit someone. I'm not really mad at the old man, I'm mad at the blood sickness. I'm mad because there's nothing we can do except wait for the worst to happen.

From Ryter's expression you can tell he regrets mentioning the cure they supposedly had before the Big Shake ruined the world. He touches a hand to his lips as if to say, you're right, let me be silent.

Lanaya looks at me and goes, "May I see her?" and so we go back into Bean's cubicle.

She's asleep, but there's a smile on her face. When she hears us enter, her eyes open and then get wider. She stares at Lanaya and says, in a hushed voice, "You're so beautiful! I've never seen anyone so beautiful. You must be from Eden."

That's my Bean, still sharper and smarter and quicker than anybody. Sick as she is, she glommed right away that Lanaya can't look so perfect and be a normal like the rest of us.

"That's right," Lanaya says, crouching by the mat. She puts her hand on Bean's forehead and says, "Where does it hurt?"

"It hurts everywhere, but only a little," Bean says almost cheerfully. "Are you my brother's luvmate?"

Lanaya laughs. "No, we're not luvmates. As a matter-of-fact, I don't think your brother likes me very much. He thinks I'm spoiled and headstrong and always get my own way."

"Lanaya brought us here," I tell Bean. "That makes up for everything else."

Lanaya gives me a funny look, but I can tell she likes what I said, and it's obvious she likes Bean. Of course you can't help but like Bean. Even a proov can't help it. Bean and Lanaya talk for a while, girl-talk kinds of things, but they don't seem to mind that I'm listening, and every now and then Bean goes, "Isn't that right, Spaz?" or, "Remember, Spaz?" and tells a lot of funny stories about what a silly googan I used to be. Pretty soon I'm laughing along with her and for some reason I'm even starting to think she doesn't look so bad. I'm thinking maybe the healer is wrong and she'll get better like she did that last time.

"I'll leave you with your big brother," Lanaya says, standing up. "I'll go help your mom prepare some edibles. You need to eat, Bean. We need to fatten you up."

"I'm not hungry anymore," she says, and my heart sinks.

When Lanaya's gone, Bean smiles at me and says, "I think she likes you. You two should get married."

"Silly girl," I tell her. "Proovs can't marry normals. And I'm not even a normal."

"You are too a normal."

"I'm a deef," I remind her. "I've got a genetic defect, remember?"

Bean sighs and settles back on her mat. "I hate that word. 'Deef.'"

"It's just a word," I tell her. "Kay told me you've been taking your remedy."

Bean looks at me. "It's only honey water and stuff to make it taste icky," she says. "It doesn't do any good."

"But you're going to be okay," I tell her.

Her skinny little hands reach out from under the blankets. They feel cool and dry and weak, like old people's hands. "I'm glad you came," she says. "I was afraid you'd never see me again, and the last thing you'd remember was me fighting with Dad, and those names he called me. You mustn't hate him, Spaz. He can't help what he did."

"I don't hate him," I say. "I don't hate anybody. You're going to get better, Bean. You have to."

"Sure, I'll get better," Bean says, but she doesn't believe it, and neither do I. "Remember how you used to tell me stories so I'd take my remedy?"

"I remember."

"Tell me a story, Spaz. Tell me a story where everybody lives happily ever after."

So I tell her stories until she falls asleep.

CHAPTER TWENTY-ONE

A Sleep Like Death

LATER THAT NIGHT, after we'd made a meal of the edibles, and Little Face entertained us all by singing a song that had only one word — you can guess the word — later that night my foster sister Bean lies back on her mat and closes her eyes.

So far she hasn't opened them again.

The healer comes and runs her hands over Bean and tells us she's entered the long sleep, and that she'll probably never wake up. Ryter says the real word is "coma," but what does it matter about words when the only person you've ever loved, and who ever loved you, is dying?

"I'm truly sorry, my boy," Ryter says, bowing his head. "This isn't what I had in mind when we began our great adventure."

He says it so gentle and kind, I have to run outside

and kick at the bullet-scarred wall. Mostly I'm mad at myself. I knew when we left the latch that Bean didn't have much of a chance if the blood sickness came back strong. So what was I thinking? That she'd get better just because I showed up? Like I was her personal cure or something? Huh? What a mope! What a googan! What a spaz!

I'm sitting on the gutter curb, thinking the world is stupid if this is what happens to the best person ever born. What's the point if you have to live behind cutwire and steel doors and be afraid of gangs and then get sick and die because normals are too numb to remember the cure? I'm thinking maybe letting the latches burn is the right idea. Let everything burn until there's nothing left but cold ashes and clear rain.

I'm there on the gutter curb for a long time when Ryter comes out with Lanaya. They sit down on either side of me. Ryter folds his hands on his walking stick and when he speaks, his voice sounds younger than usual. "We've got a new plan," he announces. "A new adventure. Would you like to hear it?"

I haven't got the energy to tell him I'm no longer interested in his "adventures," so I just shrug.

"Remember I said they used to have a cure for Bean's disease?" he begins. "Well, I got to thinking that maybe the knowledge still exists somewhere, in a slightly different form."

The old geez has my attention.

"This better be real," I tell him. "Not some story you made up for your stupid book."

Ryter sighs. "I think there's a real enough chance, but there's no guarantee. It will be dangerous and difficult. Lanaya has agreed to help."

I notice Lanaya's nose is red where she's been crying. So even proovs get red noses, which means they're not as perfect as they say.

"What can you do to help?" I ask her. "What can anybody do to help Bean?"

Ryter and Lanaya look at each other, then at me.

"We can take her to Eden," says the proov girl.

CHAPTER TWENTY-TWO

Their Terrible Swift Engines

NO SURPRISE, Charly is against it.

"Normals aren't allowed to leave the Urb for any reason," he says, his voice trembling. "'A normal entering the Forbidden Zone will be canceled immediately.' That's rule number one. We learn it as children."

"Rules are made to be broken," Ryter tells him gently.

Charly's face gets all twisted up. "Easy for you to say, old man. But this is my daughter. Why should I let you risk her life?"

When nobody says anything, Charly has to think about it. He knows she hasn't got much life left to risk. "I don't know," he mutters. "All I know is, normals don't go to Eden."

He can't or won't look at Lanaya, and when she

reaches out to touch his shoulder he moans like he's been hit by a splat gun.

"Charly?" she says. "That rule you learn as children? You're right, of course. A normal trying to cross on his own would be destroyed automatically. But there's no rule about entering while under my protection, as my guest. Whatever happens, I won't let them cancel her. You have my word."

Kay hugs Charly from behind and rests her head on his shoulder. "She's already gone from us, Charly. What harm can it do?"

He goes, "It's wrong, is all," but the fight's gone out of him and when Kay gives us the nod, he doesn't say no.

I figure we better get moving before they change their minds. Ryter comes into Bean's cubicle with me, but I don't need any help. Bean doesn't weigh much, and it's nothing at all to carry her in my arms.

Charly and Kay have gone into their own cubicle, like they can't bear to see her leave. Lanaya unbolts the locks, opens the door, and holds back the cutwire to let me pass.

"She's so thin," says Lanaya, "so very thin and pale. We'll find a way to help her. We must."

I carry Bean down the steps where we used to play Boss of the Latch, over the concrete patch where she chalked her hopskip, and into the waiting takvee. I keep hoping Bean will wake up a little, but she doesn't move even when the seat adjusts itself around her. As if waking up would take too much strength when it's all her frail little body can do to keep breathing.

"Bean?" I whisper. "Can you hear me? I'm taking you to Eden, like I promised when you were little. Keep your eyes closed until we get there, okay?"

I'm climbing back out of the hatch to check on Little Face when the ground starts shaking. Something is coming, and knowing what it is, what it must be, it makes my heart sink down into my boots. Sure enough the air thrums and then suddenly an army of jetbikes comes roaring out of nowhere, lighting the night with the flames of their terrible swift engines.

The battle is over and the Vandals are victorious.

They ride through the streets bare-chested to show off their wounds. They whoop and holler and pull along their roped-up prisoners. The Furies look small and ordinary with their hooded cloaks torn to rags and their skull masks gone. They look as if they never could have won, but then again Ryter says the defeated always look beaten and hopeless.

I look for Vida Bleek among the prisoners, but he's nowhere to be seen.

"LOT-TI! LOT-TI!" the Vandals chant. "LOT-TI GETTS! ALWAYS WINS! LOT-TI GETTS!"

Lotti Getts, the Latch Queen, shows off her winning ways by straddling two jetbikes. She waves her chetty blade high above her head in triumph. When she spots me, her victory smile widens. She makes a motion, and instantly the jetbikes go silent.

"Still here, Spaz boy? You had your chance to escape. What stopped you?"

I can't think of what to say.

"What's a-matter, boy, rat got your tongue?"

Ryter comes up behind me. "We're on a mission of mercy," he explains. "Trying to save the life of a young woman."

The Latch Queen seems amused by the idea. "And what do you want from me?" she asks. "Arms? Escort? What?"

"Nothing, my lady," Ryter says.

"You help me trap my enemy, and ask nothing in return?"

"Only what you pledged, my lady. Free passage out of the latch. After that, we're on our own."

The Latch Queen points her chetty blade at me. "You! Spaz boy! What do you have to say for yourself? Huh? Nothing? Have you gone mute?" she demands.

Ryter nudges me.

"I'm too scared to talk," I say, fighting to get the words out.

You can tell the Latch Queen likes the idea. "Scared? Scared of me, Spaz boy? Why ever should you be scared of me?" she cackles.

"I'm scared my sister will die if we don't hurry."

She snorts and makes a face, as if disgusted to hear of such weakness. "Then be off, the lot of you! Go on, get out of here!"

We're hurrying into the takvee, when the chetty blade flashes in my face and stops so close to my nose, I can smell the warm steel. "One last thing, Spaz boy," the Latch Queen says, breathing into my ear. "Be sure and tell Billy Bizmo about my victory. Tell him to think twice before he brings battle to the White Widow." She laughs, tickling me with the steel. "I gave myself that name, didn't you know? It suits me."

She raises my chin with her blade.

"Look upon this," she says, holding up a bulging sack. A velvet sack exactly large enough to hold a human skull. "Tell Billy this is what happens to my enemies. One kiss of my blade and they lose their heads!"

Her laughter follows us all the way to Eden.

CHAPTER TWENTY-THREE

If the World Were Blue

JUST BEFORE I LOST my family unit, Bean discovered the color blue. It was just this old cracked plate she found in a pile of rubble, but once she wiped off the brick dust, the color was still bright enough to shock your eyes.

"Imagine if the whole world was this color," she said to me, holding the plate up to the gray light of day. "Everything blue, even me and you. Wouldn't it be wonderful? If something was blue, you'd *have* to love it, wouldn't you? No matter what?"

It was such a Bean thing to say. But I knew what she meant.

When she tried to make Charly understand, he took the plate away and smashed it to bits. *See*, he told her, *see! It's nothing now, it doesn't exist! There's no such thing as blue, and even if there was, it wouldn't mean anything!*

And that was such a Charly thing to say. But I knew what he meant, too. He meant I was no longer part of the family unit, no matter how Bean might want it to be different. In his mind I was dust, I didn't exist.

I figure I've got a right to hate him for that, but somehow I can't. It's hard to hate someone for being stupid and afraid, and when it comes to me and Bean, Charly was so afraid, his brain sort of froze up until he couldn't think his way to what was true.

"We're coming up on the Barrier," Lanaya announces from her console. "There it is, right ahead."

We've been crossing through the Zone, going slow so the takvee can automatically disarm the mines. I'm in the back tending to Bean, but I can see the vidscreens from here. And what I see looks so strange, it makes me think my eyes have gone wrong.

The Barrier isn't a gate or a fence; it's the color blue.

"Astonishing," Ryter is saying. "I've heard about this, and have some understanding of the concept. But to actually see it — why, it takes my breath away!"

Lanaya explains that the Barrier is really this layer of what she calls "charged air" that separates Eden from the Urb. "We can pass through without feeling a thing," she says. "But because of the charged layer, very little air is exchanged between the two atmospheres. Think of Eden as a rock in the middle of a stream. Everything whirls around it."

"What's a stream?" I ask.

Lanaya turns from the console. "Are you kidding?" she asks.

"There are no streams in the Urb, my dear," Ryter tells her. "No rivers, no lakes, no ponds. No running water at all, except when it rains."

"Never mind the stream," I say. "What's the blue stuff? Is that the, um, what did you call it, 'charged air'?"

Lanaya giggles. "That's the sky, silly. The sky is blue."

"The sky is gray," I say. "Everybody knows that."

"In the Urb," she says, "because of all the smog. In Eden the sky is blue and the ground is green."

I figure she's pulling my leg. Ground is dirt or concrete, everybody knows that. I figure in Eden the concrete won't be cracked and the dirt won't stink, but why would everything be painted green? It doesn't make sense.

But I'm wrong, flat wrong. After we pass through the Barrier that separates the atmospheres, Lanaya stops the takvee and opens the hatch. "See it with your own eyes," she says. "Why I'm always happy to come home."

The three of us stand in the open hatch and look

up at the sky. It's so blue and clear, it makes my eyes water. Then I realize my eyes are weeping because they've never seen anything this beautiful. I never thought about it before, but in the Urb the sky is so close that sometimes you think you could reach up and touch it. Here in Eden the blue goes up forever and you suddenly realize that the sky is much, much bigger than the earth below. And it's more than that: Seeing so far makes you know there's a world outside the world, and a sky beyond the sky.

And the sky, well, the sky is so big, so never-ends, that it makes your brain feel bigger, too, like there's room for more ideas. But it isn't only the sky that fills my eyes. Because what Lanaya said is true: *The earth is green.* Instead of new concrete, they've got all this green feathery stuff, like a soft rug that's somehow alive.

"Grass," Lanaya explains. "Over that way is a small forest of trees. Those velvety things are giant ferns. Aren't they lovely? I've always liked ferns."

She notices how I'm looking at everything with all my might. Like I want to stick everything I'm seeing inside my brain before she pushes a button and makes it vanish.

Ryter is quiet, too. Then he sighs so deep I'm afraid he'll pass out. "I heard stories," he says, very faint. "Impossible-to-believe stories. But the reality is much, much more amazing. I swear I can smell the green! Is that possible?"

"That's the grass," says Lanaya, smiling and shaking her head. "The leaves, the trees, the ferns — they all have their own smells. Wonderful fresh smells."

"Yes," whispers Ryter. "Wonderful." Then he wraps his thin arms around me and hugs me hard. "Thank you, son," he says.

"Are you zoomed?" I ask him. "Why are you thanking *me*?"

He grins and goes, "Because if you hadn't come into my stackbox that day, I wouldn't be here now, seeing this."

I shake my head. He really is zoomed. Crazy old man, has he forgotten I went into that stackbox to rip him off?

Lanaya starts the takvee going again, but we stay up in the hatch to watch with our own eyes as the amazing sights roll by. There isn't just one color of green, either; there's endless variations. When leaves shiver in the wind, it changes. Each tree is different, each blade of grass unique, and all of it looks alive.

The thing that grabs you by the heart is how open everything is. In the Urb the sky is close, like I say, and the buildings and ruins are even closer, but you don't think about it because that's the way it is and you can't imagine it being different. Here in Eden it's as if you can see to where the world ends, or where it blends into the blue, to the place where the earth and the sky get mixed up.

My eyes are actually starting to hurt from everything they're seeing, but I don't care. All I really care about is wanting Bean to wake up. I figure just the blue alone would cure her, if only she could see it.

Lanaya says we're only minutes from our destination, but the weird thing is, we haven't seen any other proovs. "You're not supposed to," she tells us. "Eden was designed that way. Our dwellings blend into the landscape. And we learn to blend into the landscape, too. For instance, you can't see them from here, but I happen to know there are children playing in that forest over there, dressed in leaf-colored clothing."

Later the takvee runs along the edge of a stream. Which is sort of like a gutter, only clean, with water as clear as the air. Looking down, I notice the stream has a holoquarium in it, with strange-looking fish the same color as the rocks at the bottom of the stream. But what's the point of a holoquarium if the fish are hard to see?

Lanaya laughs. "Those are real fish, silly, not holoquarium images."

I'm about to tell her I never knew there was such a thing as real fish, but decide to keep my mouth shut. I hate it when Lanaya laughs at me, even when she doesn't mean any harm.

Suddenly the takvee tilts.

"What's wrong!" I exclaim.

"Nothing," says Lanaya. "We're going up a hill, is all. Oh, I forgot, there are no hills in the Urb." We keep climbing. "Actually this particular hill is more like a small mountain," Lanaya explains. "It's the highest elevation in Eden."

It's probably stupid to keep being amazed, but I don't care. Because the hills are amazing. The higher up you go, the more you can see, like you're climbing one of the old scrapers, except this is the *ground* getting higher and higher and it doesn't feel like you're going to fall off.

Beside me, Ryter sighs and goes, "No wonder they called it 'Eden.'"

"Why?" I ask him. "What does 'Eden' mean?"

"The backtimers had a legend about it," he tells me. "Eden was a paradise."

"Yeah? And what's a paradise?"

"A place very much like this," he says. "A place where you feel happy just to be there and you never want to leave."

Just then we come over the rise of the hill. The first thing I notice is the golden light of the sun, how it makes everything glow. At first I think there's another hill in front of us, or maybe what Lanaya calls a "forest," but it doesn't look like the hills and forests we've seen so far. Shapes come out of the ground and soar up as high as trees, but they aren't trees, not quite. Other shapes could be mountains except instead they're like mirrors that reflect the sky. All the different shapes are joined together, and somehow I know without being told what thing this is.

"You live here," I say to Lanaya. "This is your crib."

She gazes at the huge and beautiful thing before us, a thing that seems to grow out of the mountains and the trees and the sky, and says, very quietly, "Yes, this is my home."

"It's a palace," says Ryter in a tone of wonder.

Then he looks at me. He doesn't have to say what he's thinking, because I'm thinking it, too. If she lives in a palace, Lanaya is no ordinary proov girl.

She really is a princess.

CHAPTER TWENTY-FOUR

What the Cyber Said

RYTER SAYS I BETTER keep my mouth closed or I'll be catching flies. But I can't help it. The more I look around, the more my jaw drops open. For instance, what Lanaya calls "home" is so huge and spacious, it's almost like living outside. And each room, which Lanaya calls a "space," has a different purpose. Some are filled with light and make you feel wide awake — work spaces, and what she calls a "conversational." Other spaces are soft and shadowy, and those, she says, are for "restful thinking" or dream-rooms for sleeping.

Most of the spaces have openings or windows that look out on the green landscape, or up into the deep blueness of the sky. The floors are made of this cool slick-but-not-slippery stuff they call "marbellium," and it changes color and surface depending on who occupies the space and what their mood is. Plus you can make any wall into a fully three-dimensional holoscape simply by touching it. Then you really *do* feel like you're in any one of a thousand different landscapes, from something called Lush African Jungle to Nighttime Lunar Surface.

"Do all proovs live in this kind of splendor?" Ryter wants to know, his old geezer eyes sparkling with interest.

"Not all of them, no," says Lanaya.

Before she can explain, two adult proovs glide into the room. A male with a small, dark, pointy beard and a female with golden hair done up in thick weaves. The're both wearing sleek white tunics, and little bits of sky-colored jewelry that glint in the sun, and like Lanaya they're both perfect and beautiful. Like actors you'd see on a 3D, only better, and that makes it hard not to stare.

"This is Jin and Bree," Lanaya says, giving each of them a quick kiss and hug. "My contributors."

It turns out Jin and Bree are what normals would call "parents," but since each proov baby is genetically "improved" before conception they're called "contributors." Jin and Bree are obviously pleased to have their daughter home, but they aren't exactly happy to see us.

"Child, what have you done?" is the first thing Jin wants to know. "You can't bring normals into Eden; it's forbidden."

"We'll discuss that later," she tells him. "Right now we've got a life to conserve."

"What?"

"Out in the takvee. Quickly."

And that's how Bean came into the private palace of a future Master of Eden. We figure out the "Master of Eden" part when Bree mentions that Lanaya has been granted certain special privileges because in a few years she'll be one of the Masters who make all the decisions for the proov world.

Being a future Master explains a lot. Like her being allowed to travel into the Urb. Or distributing edibles to the normals. Or bringing us into Eden. Apparently a future Master is given what Jin calls "unlimited educational opportunities," which means she can do just about anything she wants while she's learning how to be a leader.

"That includes, of course, the opportunity to make mistakes," Jin reminds her sternly, tugging at the point of his perfect little chin beard. "And this, child, is a very big mistake."

I'll give him credit: As soon as he sees how sick Bean is, he shuts up and helps me carry her into one of the sleeping spaces. Then he and Bree fuss over

Bean as if she was their own daughter. Jin says people in Eden don't get sick this way anymore, but they do have special life-sustaining systems on hand for those injured in accidents.

"We can stabilize her," he says, much to my relief. "We can do that much."

The life-sustaining system turns out to be a sort of portable bed with a curved plexishield. The machine helps Bean breathe and it has these special light tubes that keep her fever under control, too. I ask Jin if they have a device that will make her wake up, and he gives me a sad look and says, "I don't know. I suppose it's possible. Anything is possible," and then he and Bree leave the room to make contact with what they call the Authority to discuss the situation.

The scary thing is, the life-sustaining device looks like some sort of fancy latchboss coffin. And poor Bean is so thin and pale, and her breathing is so shallow that she looks more dead than asleep.

I put my mouth on the curve of the glass cover and go, "Bean, can you hear me? This is Spaz, okay? I want you to hang on. Don't go, Bean, please?" until Ryter gently guides me out of the room.

I go, "Maybe the Authority has a wake-up device."

"Maybe," he says.

That's what I'm hoping. If they can make the sky

blue and the world green, they can wake up one small girl, right?

While we're waiting to hear what the Authority has to say, Lanaya takes us into what she calls her "thinkspace."

"Each room has a cyber-intelligence, to control the environment and so on," she tells us, "but the thinkspace is special. It's a teaching cyber. You have to be careful what you ask this cyber, because it always delivers."

At first it looks like any of the other rooms, but when Lanaya asks a question, the walls seem to dissolve and the answers appear as images. Like she'll ask, "What is Earth?" and suddenly we're floating high above this gauzy blue planet. We're still in the room with our feet on the floor, of course, but it feels like we're looking down at a planet two thousand miles below.

The illusion is so powerful and so convincing that Little Face starts to cry, and Bree volunteers to take him to the edible space and give him something she calls "cookies and milk" while Lanaya asks the cyber to give us a tour.

"Anywhere you'd like to go?" she asks Ryter. "Any special place you'd like to see?"

"What if the place no longer exists?" Ryter asks, mysteriously.

"Try it," says Lanaya with a shrug. "See if the cyber can remember."

Ryter takes a deep breath. "In that case, I've always wanted to see the Grand Canyon."

"Let it be," Lanaya says.

Suddenly we're gliding through the most amazing place I've ever seen. Even more amazing and exciting than the famous chase scene in Coley Riggins's *Battle Quest*. It's like something from another world. Mars maybe, but it was right here on Earth. The cyber-voice tells us this is the biggest canyon that ever was, until the Big Shake destroyed it. The canyon looks like a city made for giants, with thousands of pinnacles of stone much, much taller than the highest scraper ever built. The cyber tells us the canyon was created by something called "erosion," and that explains it, but I don't think anything can explain it, not really, because the canyon looks and feels too big to hold in your mind all at once. The shadows keep changing so that the place seems somehow alive, and you feel like you could stare at it for a thousand years and still not see everything.

When the cyber-tour is over, Ryter sits there weeping and gasping for breath. "Pay no heed," he tells me, wiping his eyes on his sleeve. "I never thought to see the place. My grandfather often spoke of a trip to the Grand Canyon — he'd never seen anything so magnificent — but none of his old photographs survived the Shake. So all I had were his stories and my imagination."

"How does it compare?" Lanaya wants to know. "Your imagination to the cyber-image?"

Ryter smiles. "I wasn't thinking big enough, that's for sure. And I had no idea about the colors, or the way the sky above seems to echo what lies below. Imagine something that enormous being destroyed by a mere earthquake! It's another proof of how powerful the Big Shake really was. That we puny humans survived is almost as incredible as the Shake itself, don't you think?"

"I never thought of it that way," Lanaya says, a bit uneasily. Then she turns to me and goes, "Anything you'd like to see?"

I think about it. The thing is, we're already in the most amazing place I've ever dreamed of. More like *never* dreamed of. But there is something I want to see, even if it isn't as big or grand as the Grand Canyon. "Can the thinkspace show us what's making Bean sick?" I ask.

"I don't know," Lanaya says. "Let's find out."

She speaks a few words to the cyber. A moment later a human body rises from the floor. Not a real body, of course, but a transparent version, where you can see inside. As the body turns, some of the bones and organs begin to glow, highlighting where the sickness comes from.

Leukemia, the cyber-voice says, *any of a group of neoplastic diseases of the blood-forming organs, resulting in an abnormal increase in the production of leukocytes, often accompanied by anemia and the enlargement of the lymph nodes, spleen, and liver.*

Then the body dissolves and we're inside the bloodstream, which is loaded with things that look like fat white tires. The cyber-voice tells us the tire-looking things are white blood cells, and having too many white blood cells makes the blood weak and tired. Untreated, it can lead to death.

Among the improved population, genetic extinction of the leukemia disease group was achieved in the early twenty-first century, the cyber-voice says. *Backtimer treatments involved complex chemical therapies and bone marrow transplants, specific methods that are no longer available.*

Then the blood fades away, and we're back in the thinkspace, letting the words bang around inside our brains until we understand.

For the first time since we met, Lanaya doesn't want to meet my eyes.

"It isn't fair," I say. "Proovs never get the blood sickness, so nobody bothered to remember the cure. That's what the cyber said, isn't it?"

Lanaya nods. "I'm sorry," she says.

It feels like a fist has clenched inside my head. My face is hot and my tongue is so thick with anger, it's hard to get the words out. "I don't care how perfect you are, or how beautiful. Bean is a million times better than anybody in Eden," I say. "But you're going to let her die because she wasn't 'improved' before she was born."

"I'm sorry," Lanaya says.

"I hate you," I tell her. "I hate all of you."

And then I run to the room where my sister lies in her transparent coffin, waiting to die.

CHAPTER TWENTY-FIVE

Thinking About
the Future

LATER THAT DAY we take Bean to a place they call the Primary Laboratory. Lanaya's parents — excuse me, her contributors — got permission from the Authority to bring Bean here to see if there's anything that can be done. So far, nothing has changed. Bean still lies in the long sleep, although she doesn't seem to have gotten any worse since they put her in the glass coffin.

In the backtimes they had people called "doctors" who took care of sick people, but proovs hardly ever get sick, so they have "medical technicians" instead. The med-teks mostly do stuff like patch up proovs who get injured in accidents, so they don't really know what to make of Bean. All they can do is tell the Prime-cybers to search for data about the blood sickness.

While we're waiting, Lanaya shows us around the Primary Laboratory. The Prime is where proov babies are made and "improved," which makes it the most important place in Eden. Most of the place is underground because when the proovs were first starting out, the air was still poison from all the volcanic eruptions kicked off by the Big Shake.

"The original survivors thought the radiation came from nuclear waste, and some of it did, but the worst came from within the earth itself," Lanaya explains. "The natural radiation and the volcanic gases made the air toxic for almost a century. The average lifespan of humans dropped to something like twenty years. That's when genetic engineering really came into its own. Until then, large-scale modification had been forbidden, more or less."

We're passing through the oldest part of the Prime, which has been preserved as a reminder of how bad things were right after the Shake. There are holo images of the original genetic engineering team, and all of them are wearing gas masks. In one of the images they're standing around a small crib, holding up a crying baby.

"I notice the baby doesn't have a gas mask," Ryter observes.

"That's one of the first things they improved," Lanaya says. "The ability to tolerate higher levels of toxic gases. Every child of Eden still carries that improved gene, although we no longer need it."

"And does that child still survive?" Ryter wants to know, pointing at the image of the baby.

Lanaya gives him a strange look. "That holo was taken over two hundred years ago," she says. "That's a hundred years more than the average proov lives. The First Child has been dead for a long time."

"Ah," says Ryter, as if he's satisfied some unspoken question.

Lanaya seems amused by the question. "I know you normals think we've solved the riddle of eternal life, but we haven't," she tells him. "Before engineering, certain rare humans lived for as long as one hundred and twenty years. That survival rate has been incorporated into the coding for every child of Eden, but we haven't been able to improve upon it."

"And there's no way to reverse the aging process?" Ryter asks wistfully.

Lanaya shakes her beautiful head. "Sorry, no. We can activate the genes that lengthen lifespan, but we can't reverse aging."

"So what happens when proovs get old?" he asks, as if the subject is close to his heart.

"They age gracefully," Lanaya says with a smile. "That's the best we can do."

· · ·

They let me visit with Bean, which is really sort of pointless, since she doesn't know I'm there, but for some reason it makes me feel a little better, just looking.

"If anything can be done, we'll do it," Jin promises when he finds me there, staring through the glass.

I know they're trying to help, but I'm still pretty cranked about the unfairness of it all. "So what do you care if a normal dies?" I say. "They die every single day from all kinds of disease and you don't do anything to stop *that*."

Jin gives me this wise-and-understanding look and says, "It's easy to ignore what you can't see, and most of us have never even *seen* a normal. As you know, I think it was a mistake to bring you people into Eden, but now that you're here, we feel compelled to help, if only because Lanaya wants us to."

"She's really that big a deal, your daughter?"

"Is it a big deal to be a latchboss in the Urb?"

"The biggest," I say.

"Being one of the Masters is even bigger," Jin says. "Everything that happens in Eden is controlled, ultimately, by the Masters. Masters are not chosen or elected, they're *designed* for the job. Specifically improved to have leadership qualities, and the ability to plan for the future. To plan even beyond their own lifespan. That's very important to us, thinking about the future."

"Yeah? What's so important about the future, if you're not alive to see it?"

Jin looks at me like he can't believe I don't know what he's talking about. "That was the mistake the backtimers made, not planning far enough ahead. They knew a planet-wide disaster like the Big Shake would happen eventually, but when it *did* happen, they weren't ready for it. More than a billion people perished during the Shake and in the dark times that followed. All because nobody wanted to think about the future."

"Thinking about the future may be great for proovs," I tell him. "But normals don't even have a past, let alone a future."

"Everyone has a past," he says evasively.

"You're wrong."

I tell what's happened to memories since everybody started probing. How things in the Urb seem to be getting worse and how a lot of the latchbosses are too busy probing to care. When I get to the part about Mongo the Magnificent, Jin's perfect eyes widen in horror.

"I had no idea!" he exclaims.

That's when Ryter decides to pipe up. So far, he's mostly been quiet, listening to me spout off. "There's something else we discovered," he points out, fixing his saggy old eyes on Jin. "Brain probes are made here in Eden, with your technology, and then smuggled into the Urb."

Jin quickly shakes his head. "Impossible," he says, sounding shocked. "Why would we do that?"

Ryter shrugs. "You tell me. Are there proovs who would like to see the Urb and all the people in it disappear?"

Jin grimaces uncomfortably. "I suppose there are."

"Well, if someone wanted to wipe us out, or encourage us to self-destruct, rotting our minds would be a good place to start."

"You must be mistaken," Jin says, protesting, but you can tell he's worried that it might be true.

"Take away memory — the sense of who we are — and human beings revert to animal behavior," Ryter says. "And animals are easier to exterminate than humans."

"Exterminate? What a terrible word!" he exclaims. "Why would we want to do that?"

Ryter shrugs again. He almost looks amused by Jin's reaction. "Why would you want to exterminate us? Because we still exist. Because we're a reminder of what you used to be. Because the Urb surrounds Eden. Because we're dangerous. There are plenty of reasons — take your pick."

"This can't be," Jin says to himself. "I'll go to the Authority and ask them, and if necessary the

Authority will go to the Masters. I'm sure you must be wrong."

But he doesn't sound sure. He sounds more like a man hearing something he'd rather not think about, even if he's known about it all along.

Later that same day the word comes back that the cybers have found something interesting. "Interesting" is Bree's word. To me it sounds impossible, but I want to believe it anyway.

"The cybers could find no data on the old cures," she says at first, which opens the darkness inside my heart. "Evidently it had something to do with specific amounts of very toxic chemicals, what they called 'chemotherapy,' and controlled exposure to radiation. It's a wonder anybody survived a 'cure' like that, but apparently they did, and quite successfully, too. But it doesn't matter, because we no longer have access to their ancient technologies."

"So there's nothing you can do for her," I say.

"I didn't say that," Bree says. "I said we can't replicate the backtimer cure. But the cybers have an interesting suggestion. It may be possible to give your sister an improved gene. Several improved genes, actually, that control how the body replaces blood cells."

"And that would make it better?" I ask.

"If it works," Bree says. "We won't know until we try."

"What if it doesn't work?" I ask.

Bree gives me a long, sad look. "You already know the answer to that."

She's right. I do.

CHAPTER TWENTY-SIX

The Bean
Is Back

THREE DAYS AFTER they inject her with the new and improved genes, my little sister Bean gets her own personal future.

I'm there when it happens.

At first I don't notice anything different. I'm sort of staring into the glass coffin-thing that's keeping her barely alive, thinking about stuff from when we were both little. Stupid stuff that wouldn't mean anything to anybody but me or Bean, like the time Charly caught her feeding crumbs to the rats behind our unit and she acted all surprised that he was upset and told him, "Rats are people, too." Charly demanded to know where she got such a crazy idea, and she said, "From you, Daddy." Because, see, Charly was always calling people "rats." That's when poor old Charly realized his four-year-old daughter was a whole lot smarter than he was, and on her way to being smarter than anybody else in the Urb, period.

Anyhow, there I am looking right at her and remembering stuff so hard that at first I don't even notice that she's staring back at me. Her eyes are open and she's looking at me! And not with dead or unconscious eyes, either — she's really looking hard, like she's trying to figure out what I'm thinking. And what I'm thinking is that I must be dreaming and dreading that any second I'll startle myself awake and Bean will still be in the long sleep or worse.

But I'm not dreaming. It's true. The Bean is back.

I must have yelled or cried out, because everybody comes running. Ryter and Lanaya and Jin and the med-teks who gave her the injections, they're almost as excited as I am. The med-teks because they didn't know if the gene therapy would work, and the others because they know how much Bean means to me.

The med-teks lift up the glass cover on the coffin-thing. It's not like Bean is suddenly strong enough to get up or anything. She's really weak, barely able to raise her hand and touch my face, but I don't care. Five minutes ago I thought she was a goner, and now she's back alive and whispering that she had the weirdest dream.

"I dreamed we went to Eden," she says. "Isn't that strange?"

"We did," I tell her. "We're here, and you're getting better."

Suddenly I feel really bad about being so borked off with the proovs. If it wasn't for Lanaya and her people, Bean would be dead for sure. Maybe some of them hate normals and wish we'd disappear, but they saved my little sister, so they can't be all bad.

Nobody looks happier than Ryter. The old geez is grinning so hard I'm afraid his last few teeth will fall out. His whole face is smiling, including his eyes, and he wraps his spindly arms around my shoulders and gives me a hug that takes my breath away.

"You did it, boy!" he exclaims, wheezing with excitement. "You risked your life for a fair maiden, and now she lives! Oh what a wonderful story! I can't wait to write it down! Do you realize what you've done? You've given me a happy ending!"

"But the proovs saved her, not me," I remind him. "And besides, it was your idea to come to Eden."

Ryter shakes his head. It's as if his ancient, watery gray eyes can see all the way inside me. "Oh yes, we helped along the way, Lanaya and me, and even Little Face. But it was you who started the journey, son. None of this would have happened if you didn't have the courage to imagine it first."

He's obviously zoomed, but I don't have the heart to tell him so. But I know who the real hero is, and it isn't me or even the brave Lanaya. It's an old man with a white beard and a walking stick and a heart so big it won't let him stop thinking he can change the world by writing things down in a book that no one will ever read.

Not long after Bean wakes up from the long sleep, Jin has a whispery conversation with Lanaya. They both look worried.

"As soon as your sister can be moved, we'll have to leave the Prime," she tells me later, keeping her voice down. "People are talking."

She doesn't have to explain about people talking. She means the word is spreading that a ragged band of normals have been allowed into Eden. Which may or may not be forbidden, depending on who interprets the rules. So the longer we stay at the Primary Laboratory, the more proovs become aware of our presence.

"But she's not all the way better," I remind her. "She can barely walk and she still doesn't want to eat."

"I know," Lanaya says, patting my shoulder. "Don't worry, we'll still take good care of her. But in my own spaces, away from prying eyes."

. . .

So the very next day we all leave the Prime and return to the incredible place that Lanaya calls "home." Bean doesn't remember being there, of course, and she's at least as amazed as I am by the rooms that change scenes according to your mood.

She is still pretty weak, and can't stand up for long without feeling dizzy, but she wants to know how everything works. And when Lanaya explains, Bean seems to understand, which means she's way ahead of me.

"It's a logical extension of interactive cybernetic intelligence," Lanaya tells her, "a computer that can project itself into a three-dimensional landscape. Of course these are only holoscapes. Illusions."

Bean's eyes are so bright they could light the dark. "I used to pretend something like this," she says, gazing in wonder at the purple mountains and green valleys of a holoscape called Montana. "I'd lie on my sleeping mat and imagine that I was in a completely different world."

"What kind of world?" Lanaya wants to know.

"A world without walls," Bean says. "A world where you can go outside without being afraid."

"You're describing Eden," says Lanaya.

"I guess," Bean says. "But I meant the Urb. What

it would be like if everything hadn't been destroyed. If people stopped hurting each other and grew things instead. All those green things out there."

"Grass and trees."

"It sounds so lovely, so peaceful," Bean says dreamily. "Grass and trees."

Lanaya takes Bean by the hand and leads her to a window. "That isn't a holoscape," she says, pointing. "Those are real trees, real grass."

Bean looks outside for a long time and then sighs deeply. "It's beautiful. But it might as well be a holoscape," she says.

Lanaya looks at her curiously. "Why is that?" she asks.

"Because we can't stay here," Bean says. "Can we? When I'm better, you'll send us back. Back to the gray concrete and the acid rain and the latch gangs."

Lanaya stares at the grass and the trees and then looks from Bean to me. Her eyes are shiny and fierce.

"Not if I can help it," she vows.

CHAPTER TWENTY-SEVEN

What the Boy Said

TWO IMPORTANT THINGS happened on our seventh day in Eden. The first is that Bean learned to play a game called "chess," and the second is what happened to Little Face when he first learned to talk.

The chess thing went down like this.

Lanaya and Jin are in the game space, a room that changes shape and layout depending upon the game being played — in this case, chess. Chess is one of those deals that looks real simple, but isn't. You move sixteen pieces around a board divided into sixty-four squares. Some pieces, like Drones, can only move one square at a time; others, like Crooks or Wizards, can go all the way across the board in different directions. The object is to trap the piece they call the Master.

Jin says it's an ancient game based on strategy and warfare and stuff, one of the few games to survive the

Big Shake more or less intact. There are hologram versions with animated pieces as big as human beings, if you want, but Jin says that's just a distraction, because the real game is played inside your head.

"Great players don't even need a board or pieces," he tells Bean. "They can visualize an entire game, with every possible combination of moves."

He's explaining all this as if he's just being polite — he doesn't really expect a normal like Bean to understand.

While he's talking, Lanaya moves one of her pieces and says, "Checkmate." That means she won. "I almost never beat Jin," she tells me, "but apparently he's distracted."

Jin smiles like it doesn't matter who wins, but when they start the next game he's all business, thinking so hard sometimes it takes him five minutes to move a piece. It works, because he's got Lanaya in a checkmate in exactly ten moves.

"See?" she tells me. "I told you he was good. I like to play chess for fun, but Jin takes it very seriously. He's one of the best players in Eden."

"Nonsense," he says. "There are at least six players who are better than me." But the way he smiles, you can tell he's pleased.

When Bean asks if she can play chess, too, he seems happy that she's interested. "Why don't you play with your foster brother," he suggests. "I'll act as a kind of referee, to make sure you get the moves right."

"No," I tell him. "You'd better play Bean. She could beat me easy."

Jin chuckles and shakes his head, as if amused at my stupidity. "How do you know if you haven't played?" he asks.

"Believe me, I know," I say.

So it ends up with Jin playing Bean while me and Lanaya watch. Ryter is off on his own, doing something he calls "making notes" for his book and Bree is taking care of Little Face, which both of them seem to enjoy.

Anyhow, at first Jin tries to take it easy on Bean, like he doesn't want to discourage her from trying to learn the game. Which is so complicated, he says, it takes years and years to get really good at it. So imagine his surprise when he discovers that he can't beat a twelve-year-old girl from the Urb.

"Did you really mean to do that?" he asks, perking up when she makes a particular move about five minutes into their first game.

"Uh-huh," Bean says. "You'll see."

"I'll see?" Jin chuckles to himself, like she can't possibly mean what she's saying.

Seven moves later, he finds out.

"Oh this is fun!" Bean says, knocking over one of his taller pieces.

Jin stares at the board, then he stares at her.

"Another," he says, setting up the pieces for a new game.

They end up playing for hours. Bean never does beat him again, because from then on he takes her seriously. But he's never able to beat her, either. All of their games end in what they call a "standoff," which means neither side can win. And Jin looks like he doesn't know whether to be angry or ecstatic.

"Do you see?" he demands of Lanaya. "Do you understand what happened here?"

Nobody gets a bigger kick out of seeing Jin get beat than Lanaya. "Oh, I saw what happened," she tells him. "But I can't say that I'm surprised."

"But she's a normal!" Jin exclaims.

"Yes," says Lanaya. "And a normal can't be smarter than a proov, is that what you're saying?"

Jin shakes his head as if he's confused. Confused not so much by what Lanaya said, but by his own feelings. "I try to have an open mind on these matters," he says, "but I've been playing chess since I was five years old, and she just learned the game today. How is it possible?"

"Mmm-hmm," Lanaya says, her eyes bright and knowing. "Do me a favor. Don't say anything more.

Just think about it. Think about what it means, if a girl from the Urb can beat you at your best game."

Jin starts to say something, then changes his mind. "I'll do that," he promises. "I'll think on it."

Bean gives me a look that says, "Are these people zoomed or what?"

The truth is, I've got no answer. We've been here for a week and I still don't know what it's like to be a proov, or to think like one.

Okay, here's the deal on Little Face. Like I said, Bree's spending a lot of her time taking care of him, which is sort of unnecessary, really, because he's pretty good at taking care of himself. Not that you'd know it when Bree's around. Then all he wants to do is get hugs, or make signs that he's hungry, or smile and dance around until he has her complete attention. Whatever he's doing, it's working, because not long after the chess game ends, Bree marches into the game space and makes an announcement.

"I'm adopting this child," she says, in a way that makes me think she's been working herself up to it for hours. "I've made my decision. Don't try to talk me out of it!"

Poor Jin, he's getting it from all sides. He can't win at his favorite game, his daughter's giving him the sort of advice that a parent usually gives to a child, and now his luvmate announces she's going to adopt a normal. And not just any normal, but a kid who had to raise himself, more or less like an animal. A kid who doesn't know how to talk, and never had a bath until Bree scrubbed him clean.

"Bree, Bree," Jin says, exasperated.

"Don't you 'Bree' me!" she answers right back, her eyes flashing.

"But you know the rules," he reminds her.

Bree crosses her arms. Being angry makes her even more beautiful, which means that looking at her almost takes my breath away. "What I know is that this child needs me, and I need him."

"Surely there are others who can care for him. His own people."

"He doesn't have any people!" she exclaims. "And you're not listening. *I* need *him*."

"What are you talking about?" he asks, genuinely puzzled.

"I didn't know it until I saw him standing in our doorspace, but I've missed raising a child. I love Lanaya and I know that she loves me, but she's never really needed me, not the way this child does."

"Bree! What a terrible thing to say!"

Lanaya steps in, placing a hand on Jin's shoulder.

"Father," she says, softly but forcefully, "I never call you that. It's a backtimer word we don't use. Nevertheless, you are my father, and Bree is my mother, and I love you both dearly. But what Bree says is true. I was designed to be a Master, eventually. That means I'm unusually self-reliant, even for a proov. It can't have been much fun raising me."

Bree suddenly looks crushed. Tears leak from her beautiful eyes. "I didn't mean it that way," she says. "You were a lovely child, Lanaya. It was fascinating watching you grow up. I wouldn't trade it for anything."

Lanaya rushes to embrace her. "Oh, Mother, dear, I know you love me. But I understand. I really do."

Bree wipes at her tears and laughs. "You've always understood, Lanaya, almost from the moment you were born. I've often felt like you were the contributor and *I* was the child."

"Enough!" says Jin. "Both of you, please! The problem isn't with either one of you. The problem is with the child! It simply won't be allowed, no matter how much you say you care for him. And as to what the child really wants, we can't know that, can we? Because he can't tell us."

Jin crosses his arms, as if he thinks he's had the final word on the subject. But he hasn't, not quite.

Because that's the exact moment when Little Face decides to start talking.

"I love Bree," the little boy says, as fierce as a latchboss declaring war. "I love Bree and Bree loves me."

And that pretty much settles the question.

CHAPTER TWENTY-EIGHT

When They Come for Us in the Apple Trees

IT'S NOT LIKE LITTLE FACE suddenly turned into a chatterbox or anything. He still doesn't talk much. Only when it's very important and he can't make himself understood any other way. Bree says Little Face isn't a proper name and when he gets a little older she'll help him choose a real name. Jin pretty much keeps out of it, although I notice he's started to treat the boy like his own child. So maybe it will all work out, if they can figure out how to get around the rules.

Meanwhile me and Bean and Ryter spend a lot of our time outside. We discovered that the coolest thing in the world is to walk on grass in our bare feet. Grasswalking. It feels sort of tickly and smooth and alive somehow, even though it's just this green stuff that grows out of the ground. Bean says she's never seen anything so beautiful, and that the only things she likes as much as grass are the flowers and trees, and maybe the blue sky.

"Did they have these things before they invented Eden?" she wants to know.

"Oh yes, I think so," Ryter tells her. "They say that before the Big Shake, trees grew right in the middle of the Urb. Grass and flowers, too."

Bean smiles and shakes her head. She thinks maybe it's just backtimer talk, but she's too polite to say so.

In my opinion what's happened to Bean is even more amazing than the stuff that grows out of the ground. Her skin is no longer pale or sick-looking. She's strong enough to run and jump and turn cartwheels, which she hasn't been able to do since she was, like, five years old.

"I'm a new me," she brags. "New and improved."

"Don't let the proovs hear you say that," I warn her. "They think they're the only ones who are improved."

We're walking, all three of us, along what they call a "brook." A brook is like a river only smaller, and if you stick your bare feet in the clear, cool water, it feels good. Ryter says sticking his old feet in the water makes him feel younger, even though the water makes you wrinkle after a while.

"How come you're always talking about being old?" Bean wants to know.

"Because I *am* old," Ryter says. "I don't really mind the 'old' part. I'm just worried I won't have enough time to finish my book."

Bean nods wisely, as if she expected that particular answer. "But would it ever really be finished?" she asks. "I thought the book was your life, and it would only end when your life ends. Except it won't really end, because people will read it and remember, so in a way you'll live forever."

At first I think he's offended, but after a while a smile slowly creases his aged face. "Thank you, Bean," he says, and pats her hand.

"For what?"

"For reminding me of why I'm a writer."

They come for us one day while Bean and me are climbing apple trees. An apple is this truly delicious edible that actually grows on trees, and it always tastes better if you pick it yourself. The only thing better is if your best friend picks it for you.

Bean finds the best apple in our tree and hands it up to me. "You know what this tastes like when you first bite into it?" she asks.

"No, what?"

"Blue sky."

"You're zoomed."

"You ever eat blue sky?"

"No," I admit.

"Try it sometime," she says. "It's apple-flavored."

There's no arguing with Bean when she gets hold of a silly idea, so I don't bother trying. Besides, I kind of like the idea. I'm also thinking it would be cool if we could just stay in the tree and never come down. Which is probably at least as zoomed as thinking that the sky tastes like apples.

We talk about everything while we're up in the tree munching on apples. Stuff from when we were kids, and dumb things Charly said, and what it was like after I got banished, and my adventures with Ryter and the boy, and the rats in the Pipe, everything. Except one thing: We don't talk about what will happen if we have to return to the Urb. We don't want to think about it, let alone talk about it. Because once you've felt grass under your feet and tasted blue sky, well, you never want to go back.

We're counting clouds when they come for us. At first we think it's one of the clouds, the way it floats through the air. But as the thing gets closer it looks something like a floating takvee without the armor. Except unlike a takvee, it doesn't make any noise, just a soft whoosh as it passes through the air.

Later I find out it's called a skydee, for Sky Flight

Device, and it works on some sort of magnetic repulsion deal. I'm thinking maybe Lanaya arranged to give us a ride, so we can see Eden from the air. But it's not it at all. Not even close.

The skydee comes to a gentle stop beneath the apple trees, hovering just above the grass. The little craft opens, and two proovs get out. Big male types designed to have extra muscles. And unlike most proovs, they're not dressed in white tunics. They're wearing what looks like security uniforms. Enforcers.

They stand under the apple tree and look up at me. One of them goes, "Are you the normal called Spaz?"

"Yes."

"You and your companions have been summoned by the Masters. You must come at once."

Apparently they don't trust us to obey, because when me and Bean get down from the tree, they place us in body-cuffs and take us away, as if we're criminals.

Which, as it turns out, we are.

CHAPTER TWENTY-NINE

Say Good-bye
to Eden

SO WE GET TO FLY in the skydee, but it isn't much fun. The enforcers shove us down into the bottom of the vehicle where we can't see anything, and when Bean starts to complain, they go, "Silence!" in a way that makes my stomach melt, so we both shut up until we get there.

"There" is a place called Stadium. Only it's nothing like the ruins of the old stadiums in the Urb, which are huge piles of crumbling concrete and rusted steel. Stadium is really a small, curving hillside that looks like it was scooped out by a giant spoon. When we get there, the green hillside is already covered with people — proovs, of course — and the enforcers tell us they've all been summoned, too, just like us.

"So they all arrived in body-cuffs?" I ask, and one of the enforcers looks at me like I'm some sort of talking animal, not worth answering.

The enforcers release the body-cuffs, and Bean and me stumble into this smooth black circle at the bottom of the hillside. The surface under our feet is polished like a dark mirror, but not slippery somehow.

Ryter is already in the black circle, waiting for us. He's holding his walking stick and standing tall in a fresh white tunic. His white beard ruffles in the breeze, and he looks fierce and proud and very old all at the same time.

"Don't leave the circle," he warns us. "The edges are charged, and you'll get a rude shock."

"Ryter!" I say. "What's going on?"

Ryter gazes up at the gathering crowd of proovs. There's barely an empty space on the hillside. What makes it really weird is, before this we haven't ever seen more than five or six proovs in the same place at the same time. Now there are thousands of them out there. We hear the murmur of their voices, and we can almost feel the force of thousands of proovs staring at us, wanting to know who we are and how we dared enter Eden.

"What's going on? Judgment Day is here," Ryter says. "A kind of trial, I assume."

"Trial? What's a trial?"

"From the backtimes," Ryter explains. "It was a

way of deciding if you broke the rules, and what the punishment should be if you did."

The latchbosses make all those decisions in the Urb. And since a latchboss also makes his own rules, you never really know until you've broken one, and then it's too late.

"They have a different way of enforcing things here," Ryter says. "Jin explained it when they came for me. It seems we've been found in violation of the rule forbidding normals in Eden. Apparently most proovs think we should be banished, and the sooner the better. But before a judgment can be made, all the people of Eden must hear the evidence, make recommendations, and then bear witness to the final decision of the Masters."

"Where's the boy?" Bean wants to know, looking anxiously around. "Where's Little Face?"

"Hidden away," Ryter says, keeping his voice low, and making a sign that we should speak no more about it.

So Bree hasn't given up on her promise to raise him like one of her own. Which makes me like her even more than I did before.

"What about Lanaya?" I ask.

"She's in trouble, too," Ryter says. "She'll have to answer to the Masters."

All of a sudden a hush falls in Stadium as the gathering proovs go silent. They're all staring at something beyond us, and I turn in time to see what they're watching.

Right behind us a small hill is coming unhinged.

I swear, that's what it looks like. A section of grass tilts up like a lid, then a circular platform rises out of the ground. The platform seems to be made out of the same mirrored black surface we're standing on, but the shape of it changes and expands as it rises. Then when the whole thing has unfolded from the ground, the platform slowly pivots around until it faces Stadium.

On the platform, seated in transparent thrones, are the seven Masters of Eden. I know without being told who they are. They seem to radiate power and authority without saying a word, or making a threat.

Some of the Masters are young, but at least four of the seven are quite old. They don't look geezer-old like Ryter, with his wrinkled skin and missing teeth, but they have the fragile appearance of old age. Even the very old ones still look perfect somehow, as if age has sharpened their focus on being alive.

Standing before them, looking beautiful and angry but not afraid — never afraid — is our friend Lanaya. I try to catch her attention, but she seems to be avoiding my eyes on purpose, like she doesn't want to be distracted.

The oldest Master rises from her transparent throne and thumps the platform with a long black stick.

"Future Master Lanaya, to the charge of bringing normals into Eden, what say you?"

Lanaya faces the hillside, as if she wants to respond to the people there, and not just to the Masters.

"What say you?" repeats the old Master.

Lanaya takes a deep breath and speaks in a voice that somehow carries to the far ends of Stadium. "I say if saving lives is against the rules, then the rules must be changed!"

The oldest Master thumps her stick impatiently. "Explain," she demands.

"They saved my life, so I helped save one of theirs."

"Tell your entire story, child," the old Master urges. "Don't make us drag it out of you piecemeal."

Lanaya bows to the old woman. "My thanks to you, Master Ryla. I'm aware that you've taken a special interest in me, since I will one day sit where you sit, and listen as you have listened. I only hope I can do as good a job as you have done."

"Don't bother trying to charm me, child," snaps

the ancient proov. "I'm too old to be charmed, even by one so charming and persuasive as yourself. So get on with it."

Lanaya grins and bows again. "My apologies. Let me begin by telling you — all of you" — she says, raising her hand to the gathered proovs — "that many times I have crossed the Zone and journeyed into the Urb. Sometimes to trade, as some of you have also done, but more often to study the people who live there. The unimproved. The human beings we so contemptuously refer to as 'normals.'"

From the crowd come murmurs of comment and exclamation. I can see many of them shaking their heads, frowning in disapproval.

"Such journeys are, as all of us know, discouraged, and for good reason," Lanaya admits. "There are many dangers in the Urb. Violence, disease, toxic smog. But the greatest danger is ignorance. I speak not only of the ignorance of the normals, but of our own ignorance. We despise the very idea of being 'normal,' and yet those who are normal do not despise us for our apparent 'perfection.'"

She pauses, as if she wants to let that sink in, but I don't see many of the proovs nodding in agreement.

"Lately there are new dangers in the Urb," she continues, pacing about the stage. "In some of the latches the leaders have stopped leading. Anarchy reigns. Mobs run wild, burning and looting. And why have the leaders failed? Because we have supplied them with brain probes!"

Master Ryla bangs her stick. "Do you have proof of this treachery?" she demands, her ancient eyes flashing.

"I do," Lanaya says. "Mindprobes have long been forbidden in Eden, because we know the dangers. And yet there are those who encourage the spread of probing in the Urb. At first I didn't know why this should be. And then the truth of it was explained to me by one of the normals you see before you."

She points to Ryter. He bows his head slightly.

"That old man may not have benefited from genetic improvement, but he knows what he knows. He knows there are those in Eden who wish to see the normals destroyed. And what better way than to encourage them to destroy themselves with brain-rotting mindprobes?"

Many of those on the hillside rise to their feet. Some of them are shouting, although I can't quite make out what they're saying.

Again, Ryla thumps her black stick. All fall silent.

"We will investigate," she says, in a voice as clear as an old, true bell. "If what you say is true, we will take appropriate action. But what has this to do with bringing normals into Eden? What has this to do with saving your life, and you saving one of theirs?"

Lanaya explains about her takvee getting surrounded when she was trying to pass out edibles to the starving mob. She tells how Ryter risked his own life to distract the mob while she got away. Then she points to me. "And this normal, a boy with no parents, a boy shunned even by the lowest of the low, this boy risked his life not only to save me, but to save his sister, who was dying. How could I refuse to help when I knew she might be saved if only I could bring her here?"

There are a few murmurs of agreement from the assembled proovs, but not many.

"As you can see, she was easily cured by our technology. We have the means to cure almost all of the diseases that plague the Urb, and yet we don't bother trying! We let them sicken and die. We let them starve; we let their latches burn. Is that right? Is that proper? I say no! I say we must remember that the people we call 'normal' are not so different from ourselves!"

Heckling comes from the crowd on the hill. Lanaya has gone too far. "Look at them!" someone cries. "They're ugly! They're hideous! They're stupid! They're *normal*!"

Lanaya waits until the shouting dies down and then raises her hand, pointing to her own beautiful face. "Is this how we judge ourselves? By our pretty faces? By perfect noses? Delicate ears? Lustrous hair? Is that why the First Engineers risked their lives to improve our chances of survival?"

More shouting from the crowd. "Don't forget brains, Lanaya! We're smarter, too!"

Lanaya smiles to herself, as if that's exactly the comment she hoped to inspire. "Smarter? Is that what makes us proovs?"

"YES!" they shout. "YES!"

Ryla thumps her black stick. "Let her speak!" she roars.

Lanaya makes a bow of thanks to the old Master. "We come to the subject of intelligence," she says, "because all of us believe we're smarter than any normal. That makes it easier for us to pretend they're not really human, like us. But what if I told you that a normal, a girl of twelve, learned the game of chess in less than an hour, and then beat one of the top-rated players in Eden?"

The sounds coming from Stadium mean that no one believes her. They think it impossible that a girl from the Urb could be smarter than a man born in Eden.

"Think about it, people!" Lanaya shouts, making

herself heard above the roar of disbelief. "Where do we come from? Our genetic coding is the same! We're all human beings! We all start from the same place, the children of the Urb! And some of the Urb children don't need any improvement! They're already smart! Already intelligent! Already gifted! If nothing else, they have the gift of courage!"

"NO!" the crowd roars. "NO!"

"Yes!" Lanaya shouts, raising her fists. Then she points at me and Bean. "Yes! Let these young normals be raised in Eden, with all of our advantages, and they'll do more than beat us at chess! They'll teach us what it truly is to be human! Because they have already experienced something none of you have: They risked everything simply to go on living!"

"NO!" the crowd roars. "NO!"

"Yes! Yes!" Lanaya shouts. She points at Ryter. "See this old man? He's lived but half as long as some of you, and yet he has more courage, more imagination than *any* of you! He *must* have, simply to survive! Let him teach us! Let him tell us his stories! Let him write that the children of Eden have opened the gates to paradise!"

The crowd roars back, drowning her out. The old Master thumps her black stick. A hush of silence finally descends upon Stadium. "Stay if you agree!" Ryla commands. "Leave if you don't."

Proovs by the thousands stream off of the hillside, leaving it green and empty.

Lanaya stares at the vanishing crowds as if she can't believe her own eyes. "Masters," she finally calls out in a much smaller voice. "What say you?"

The Masters quietly confer among themselves for many minutes. Once or twice they look over at the three of us, but their perfect faces give nothing away.

When they are done, Ryla thumps her stick three times and then slowly walks to the front of the platform. "Lanaya, you spoke well," she says. "When you are a Master, things may change. But for now the rule must stand. Eden shall be Eden. The Masters have spoken."

Then she turns her back and walks away.

CHAPTER THIRTY

The Sound
of Jetbikes

FIVE HOURS LATER, me and Ryter are back in the stacks, and the idea of Eden is already like a dream that starts fading the instant you wake up.

The way it went down, we never even had a chance to thank Lanaya for all she did, for helping to save Bean and everything. Because as soon as the old Master finished thumping her stick, the enforcers shoved us into a takvee and, before you could say "proovs always win," we were rolling through the Zone.

First stop was Bean's latch, and they never even let me out to say good-bye. All Bean had time for was a quick kiss on my cheek and a whispered promise: "I'll see you again even if I have to walk the Pipe myself." Then she was gone and the takvee was already accelerating, heading back into the Zone. From there we crossed into Billy Bizmo's latch, and the fancy proov-built takvee delivered us right to the stackbox where it all started.

"Home sweet home!" Ryter exclaims when he sees the rotten little cubicle where I ripped him off the first time. The weird thing is, he's not kidding; he really is happy to be back in his old stackbox.

"Mind you, I could have lived my final days in Eden, living the life of luxury, and the smile never would have left my face. But who would finish my book?" he says. "Huh? What's to write about if life is perfect? If you spend all of your time lazing about and dangling your old feet in cool streams of clean water? Writers need a challenge. They need to struggle. They need to fight."

He's looking over at where I'm crouched, back against the wall, chin on my knees. The little stackbox is almost empty, everything gone but the old crate he used for a desk and the thick pile of loose paper he calls a "book." The place smells old, and I hate it. The whole Urb smells old and used up, and I hate that, too.

Ryter sees what I'm thinking, and sinks creakily down beside me. He strokes his scraggly white beard thoughtfully and then goes, "Don't let the darkness eat you up, son. Think what you accomplished. You wanted to save your sister, and you did. Everything else was extra. Think of it as an experience you'll never forget. Why, you've seen blue sky and green grass. And that blue sky is inside your mind, boy! It's there forever! Can't be erased!"

I groan and bury my face in my heads. "Yeah?" I mutter. "What if I want to forget everything? And what does it matter if I remember?"

"What does it matter?" he asks, sounding astonished. "Are you zoomed, boy?"

"It just seems so unfair."

"Let me remind you. Bean is alive. Little Face is saved. Is that unfair?" he demands. "Is it?"

"No."

"Then get used to it. You must remember the past because it brings you here, to the right now, today, this moment, and from here you can look to the future. A possible future I never even imagined until we went on our great adventure. I won't get a chance to see that future, but you will."

"You're not that old," I say. "So shut up about dying, okay?"

Ryter puts his withered hand on my shoulder and says, very quietly, "It's not old age that's going to kill me, son."

"What are you talking about?"

He sighs, and you can tell he's been thinking about this for a while. "Look," he says, trying to explain, "when things go wrong, outsiders get blamed, and writers tend to be outsiders. That was true in the backtimes and it's true now, when I'm the only writer left in the world."

I look over at him. For some reason there's a lump in my throat. "But why? Why should anybody care about an old pile of papers? If nobody reads, why should they care what you write?"

He shrugs. "I guess it's better than not caring," he says. "I don't have any of the answers, son. Never did. All I can do is keep asking the questions. Keep trying to make sense out of why people do what they do."

"Yeah? Well, I wish I'd never been born."

"Really?" he asks, like he wants to know. "Why is that?"

"'Cause Billy Bizmo is going to make me wish I'd never been born, that's why. Because I broke his stupid rules."

"Ah," Ryter says. He leans in closer and his voice is old and soft and full of the things he knows. "You've nothing to fear from Billy Bizmo, son. You never did."

"Oh, yeah? Why is that?"

He looks at me curiously. "You haven't figured it out yet, have you?"

"Figured out what?"

"Why he's taken a special interest in you."

I don't know what he's talking about. It doesn't make any sense. Billy doesn't care any more about me than he does about any of the other things he owns. Luxury items, mindprobes, weapons, warriors, Spaz boy, we're all the same. We just belong to him, like everything else in his latch.

"Rest easy," Ryter suggests. "Things will look better in the morning."

Yeah, right. Kay, my former foster mom, she used to say the same thing. It was stupid then and it's stupid now. Things never look better in the morning. How could they, when nothing ever changes? But I'm tired of thinking, tired of trying not to remember, and pretty soon I drift off, and then I'm falling asleep, kind of drifting down into the darkness.

"Easy," an old voice whispers. "Easy."

When I wake up hours later, there's a roaring inside the dark.

Jetbike engines, coming this way. And I know in my heart they're coming for us.

CHAPTER THIRTY-ONE

Fear
Itself

THE LATCH IS BURNING. From high atop the stackboxes we can see the fireglow lighting up clouds of smoke along the dark horizon. The clouds look like angry mouths biting holes in the night.

The jetbikes roar like an acid-rain storm, coming closer and closer. There's another sound, too, a kind of high-pitched moaning that follows the jetbikes. *Ooohhh . . . oooohhh . . .* like an evil wind. A furious wind.

Standing beside me, Ryter says, " 'Things fall apart; the center cannot hold; mere anarchy is loosed upon the world.' " Then he grunts to himself, as if remembering something important. "That's from a poem," he explains. "Yeats. The poet himself is long forgotten, but some of his lines live on. Thought I knew what it meant, all these years, but I had it wrong. Now I know."

"We'd better run," I tell him urgently. "They're coming this way."

"Of course they're coming this way," he says, as if speaking to himself.

The night blazes in his sky-gray eyes. I tug at his sleeve. "Come on!"

Gently he frees himself from my grasp. "Ssssh," he says. "There's nothing to fear."

"What are you talking about?" I plead.

"'Nothing to fear but fear itself,'" he says. "That's from another poem, I think. Or was it a speech? Can't recall."

"Ryter, we've got to get out of here right now!"

When he turns to me, his face looks peaceful and oddly young. "Listen to me, son. My running days are over. And if I did run away, others would be hurt."

"You're zoomed!" I cry. "Come on, you stupid old geez! We can run for the Pipe! They'll never find us. Let 'em burn the whole latch, what do we care! We'll just keep running and running! We'll have lots more adventures and you can write them down in your book!"

"Ssshh," Ryter says. "Hush."

Suddenly the jetbikes swarm into the stackboxes, splitting the air with their furious roaring. Headlights scorch the sky like laser beams, and somewhere close by a baby starts to cry.

This is the end, I'm thinking, the end the end.

Must be a hundred jetbikes swarming fast and deadly. The jetbikers howl, firing splat guns in the air as the mob follows them into the stackboxes. A mob like we saw in Mongo's latch. More animal than human. Shrieking and howling, ripping apart anything they can get their hands on.

They see Ryter standing high on the stackboxes, and they shriek his name. "WHEEL HIM! WHEEL HIM!"

No, I'm thinking, no. But there's nothing I can do, no way to stop the furious, mindless wave that breaks over the stackboxes. A wave of fists and snapping teeth and empty eyes.

"Save my pages!" Ryter yells to me as the hands grab hold and suck him down into the mob.

I try to save them, I do. In the light-exploded darkness I crawl into his stackbox on my knees and gather up the pages of his book. Trying to stuff them under my shirt, close to my heart. But there are so many pages that some get loose and drift away like the falling leaves of Eden.

Empty faces glitter with glee, finding my fear. Snatching pages out of the air. Tearing the pages to pieces. Stuffing the pieces in their bloody mouths as they scream, "WHEEL! WHEEL! WHEEL!" and then hands rip open my shirt and seize the rest of Ryter's book, feeding pages to the fire that follows them everywhere.

The pages burn and burn and burn.

"No!" I'm screaming. "Don't!" but they're not listening. They can't listen. They don't know how.

Hands grab me and carry me away and throw me to the ground. I'm spitting out dirt and trying to get my breath when someone speaks my name.

"Spaz boy! Is that you?"

When I roll over on my back, I'm looking up at Billy Bizmo. He's got a chetty blade in one hand and a splat gun in the other, and his eyes are alive with the fire.

"Stop them!" I beg him. "He's just an old man!"

Billy uses his chetty to clear a space. The mob backs off a few feet and he's able to get to me. At first I think he's going to cut me with the chetty, but that's not it. He wants to tell me something.

"Nothing I can do, Spaz boy. Those proov enforcers that brought you back? They deactivated all the probes."

"What?" I gasp.

"Ruined the whole deal. Mindprobes don't work anymore. You can still stick the needle in your brain, but nothing happens."

Now I get it, why the latch is burning, why the jet-bikes have come. Because the probes have been destroyed and somebody has to take the blame. We were with the proovs, so it must be our fault.

"WHEEL!" the mob shrieks. "WHEEL!"

They've tied a rope around the old man's waist. He's not struggling or anything, his eyes look like he's already a long ways from here. Someplace clean and peaceful and quiet. Someplace where the sky is blue.

"Ryter!" I scream out, but he can't hear me or see me.

Then I'm begging Billy Bizmo. "You're the latch-boss, you can stop them!"

Billy does a weird thing. He puts his chetty blade on the ground and reaches out and touches the side of my face. "Sorry, kid. No one can stop a mob when it wants blood. Not even me."

"You didn't even try!"

"I did what I could, Spaz boy. They could have blamed you. I made sure it was the old man."

"But why? Why him and not me?"

Billy shakes his head as if he can't believe I'm so stupid. "Because you're my son," he says.

CHAPTER THIRTY-TWO

The Last Book in the Universe

YOU'RE MY SON.

The truth of it explodes inside my head and turns me upside down and inside out. I don't know my name, or who I am. I don't know anything. All I know is, I'm running away from Billy Bizmo. Running into the mob, fighting my way to the old man. Screaming for them to stop, it wasn't his fault, please stop.

The crowd melts enough so I can see what's happening. They've tied the rope to the back of a jetbike, and Ryter is hobbling along, trying to keep up.

I try to call his name, but nothing comes out. All I can do is follow as they wheel him through the stacks. The mob chanting, "DO IT! DO IT!" but the jetbikers are taking their time.

People from all over the Urb have come to see

them wheel the old man. They want to punish Ryter for all the bad things that have ever happened, and I see from their faces that Billy's right. No one can stop what's going to happen.

A couple of times I try to grab him and undo the drag ropes, but the Bangers keep shoving me off. They think it's funny, me trying to free a wheeler. Part of the game. Their eyes are dead cold because they can't feel anything, and if I'm not careful, they'll wheel me, too.

I don't care if they do.

"Don't risk it!" the old man warns me when I make a move. "You're my only hope!"

"But they burned your pages!" I cry, running after him. "Your book! They tore it up and burned it! I tried but I couldn't stop them."

Ryter looks back at me and smiles. "The pages don't matter," he says. "You're the book now! You're the last book in the universe! Make it a good one!"

The Bangers finally get bored and decide to end it. They gun their engines. The drag rope yanks at Ryter and he falls, his frail body spinning away from me.

They wheel the life out of him, then, until there's nothing left but a bundle of rags, and the broken bones of my old friend. But I'm not there at the very end. My brain won't let me see it, not the worst part.

The last thing I remember is running after the jet-bikes and then the smell of lightning fills my nose, the clean electric smell that comes after a thunderstorm, and the blackness rises up and takes me down.

CHAPTER THIRTY-THREE

Spaz
No More

WHEN I FINALLY WOKE UP, the mob was gone and the fires had burned out. The whole latch felt empty, but I could see people hiding in the shadows, biding their time until it was safe again. As safe as it ever gets in the Urb.

I thought about running away. I thought about following the Pipe to the end of the world. And then I thought about what Ryter said, and I went back to his empty stackbox, but there was nothing left, not even a scrap of paper. So I walked through vacant streets where the buildings were taller than daylight. I walked through burned-out blocks that still smoldered, and empty ruins that even the rats had left behind. I walked until I found myself at the Crypts, the concrete bunker where the Bully Bangers live, and I went to my cube and stayed there, watching old 3Ds and trying not to remember. Staring at the walls and trying not to remember. Sleeping and trying not to remember.

Nothing worked. I kept remembering.

Once a Banger came and told me Billy Bizmo wanted to see me, but I said forget it, and then one day Billy himself came down and told me how my mother had died when I was born, and he'd put me with a family unit because it was no good growing up with a latchboss for a dad, and he hoped someday I'd understand about that, and about everything else, too.

"I understand I never want to be like you," I said, and he went away and left me alone.

Later that night I did a really strange thing. I went down to the pawn mart and found this old voice-writer in a tronic junkpile, covered with dust. There's a lot of gizmos you have to attach, but basically you talk in one end and words come out the other. And so I started talking about the old man, and all the things he told me, and how he helped me run the latches and save Bean and everything, and after a while I sort of figured out what he meant about me being the last book in the universe.

They call me Ryter now, like they called him.

And then one night I wake up in the dark and know I'm not alone.

"Who's there?" I say to the darkness.

A latch runner speaks from the shadows. "I'm not here," he says. "We never met, understood? All I am is a message."

"What message?"

"A message from Eden," he says. His voice sounds like the whisper of wind in a clear sky. *"Someone you know says, 'Chox!' and 'Don't forget me!' and 'Thank you!' and a whole lot more. He grows a little every day and we love him as our own. Do not despair, my friend. Today is theirs, but the future is ours."*

Long after the runner vanishes, I can hear Lanaya's message echoing in my head. Especially the last part about the future being ours.

Yes, I'm thinking, yes, I'm writing, yes, yes, yes.

AFTER WORDS™

RODMAN PHILBRICK'S

The Last Book in the Universe

CONTENTS

After Words™ guide by Anamika Bhatnagar

About the Author

After years of writing mysteries and suspense thrillers for adults, Rodman Philbrick decided to try his hand at a novel for young readers. That novel, *Freak the Mighty*, was published in 1993 to great acclaim. In addition to being named an ALA Best Book for Young Adults and winning several state awards, it was also made into the Miramax feature film *The Mighty* in 1998. Rod returns to *Freak the Mighty* protagonist Maxwell Kane's story in a sequel, *Max the Mighty*, a fast-paced cross-country odyssey.

Rod takes young readers to the American West in his exhilarating tale of two brothers on the run, *The Fire Pony*, winner of the Capital Choice Award, and on to a land where nothing is as it seems in the science-fiction adventure *REM World*. After completing *The Last Book in the Universe*, also an ALA Best Book for Young Adults, Rod thought back to his New England roots and knowledge of boat-building to write *The Young Man and the Sea*, the story of a boy who tries to save his family by catching a giant bluefin tuna. *School Library Journal* praised the novel's "wide-open adventure" and "heart-pounding suspense" and named it a Best Book of the Year in 2004.

Rodman Philbrick has also written several spine-tingling series for young readers with his wife, Lynn Harnett, including The House on Cherry Street and The Werewolf Chronicles. Rod and Lynn divide their time between homes on the coast of Maine and in the Florida Keys.

Writing for the Future: An Interview with Rodman Philbrick

Q: *What inspired you to write* The Last Book in the Universe?
A: The editor Michael Cart asked me to contribute a story to an anthology called *Tomorrowland*. At first all I came up with was an intriguing title, "The Last Book in the Universe." Then I had to think up a world where there might be a "last book," and think about why people had stopped reading. After finishing the short story, which was eventually published, I couldn't stop thinking about Spaz's world and set about making it a full-scale novel. No doubt many of the "sci-fi" elements came from my love of movies like the original *The Time Machine*, and from my adolescent fascination with comic book adventures.

Q: *We've included the original short story in this book (it's on page 233). What did you do to expand it into a novel?*
A: The short story is pretty much confined to Spaz and Ryter. To make it an interesting novel I needed more characters and more adventure. So I invented Eden and populated it with people who had "improved" themselves genetically. Then I added Spaz's sister Bean, put her in peril, and the adventure began.

Q: *Spaz is different from most of the people we meet in the Urb. In part, it's because he doesn't use mindprobes because of his epilepsy, but there's something else that sets him apart as well. What do you think that is?*

A: Spaz is an outsider, so he's more able to think for himself and see the world with clear eyes. He's open to people, as he hopes they'll be open to him.

Q: *Is Ryter based on a real person?*
A: Ryter is an older and much braver version of myself — an improved me that looks like Sean Connery!

Q: *Life is obviously very different for humans after the Big Shake, but do you see any parallels between Spaz's world and our own?*
A: Oh, yes. There are versions of the latches in many urban areas today. Various addictive drugs do as much damage to the brain as the mindprobes. And of course we've embarked on the dangerous and exciting adventure of investigating the process of genetic engineering. No one knows how far it will go, or if the human race will eventually take control of its own evolution.

Q: *Our society is fixated on makeovers and plastic surgery. Aren't we already on our way to creating proovs?*
A: Yes. Take a walk through Beverly Hills and you'll see them everywhere.

Q: *Speaking of proovs, the characters in this book use a lot of words that aren't part of our vocabulary. How did you come up with them?*
A: As a teenager I was fascinated by the Anthony Burgess novel *A Clockwork Orange*. He made up words that are a combination of Russian and English. It added to the whole flavor and feeling of the story. I tried to do a similar thing by inventing words that might be useful in my own future world.

Q: *Ryter makes a few references to* The Odyssey *while he and Spaz are traveling across the latches. How is their journey similar?*

A: The warrior Odysseus is trying to get home to his wife and family. He repeatedly risks his life to try and find his way home. Spaz's family is one person — his stepsister Bean — and he'll do anything to help her. Spaz isn't as courageous as Odysseus, and he certainly isn't a great warrior, but Ryter recognizes the similarities and comments upon it.

Q: *You've written books that are based in a familiar setting, like* Freak the Mighty, *and others that take place in lands you've invented, like this book. Which is easier to write about?*

A: Imagined worlds are always a bit more difficult for me. I can't write about a place until it seems real in my own head, so that obviously takes a leap of imagination that's not required for the real world.

Q: *Your most recent novel,* The Young Man and the Sea, *also involves an epic journey of sorts. What can you tell us about it?*

A: It's the story of Skiff Beaman, a kid who sets out in a very small boat at night, alone, and journeys thirty miles out to sea to try and harpoon a giant bluefin tuna.

Q: *Can you imagine a world without fishing? What would you do in your free time?*

A: Is there anything but fishing and being out on the water? Well, yes, actually. I have to keep the boat in good repair so it doesn't sink! Luckily I'm good with my hands.

New Words for a New World

Rodman Philbrick created a whole new way of talking for Spaz and the people of the Urb. Here is a selected glossary:

3D: a holographic movie that's considered old technology compared to a mindprobe

backtimes: the time before the Big Shake, the cataclysmic earthquakes that destroyed civilization

bork off, to: to irritate

bristlebar: a protective device

cancellation: death

carboshake: a beverage that provides energy

chetty blade: a machete knife

choxbar: a prepackaged food item that tastes like chocolate

contributors: what proovs call their birth parents

crib: a room or a home

cut someone's red, to: to kill someone

cutwire: a protective device similar to barbed wire

cyber-intelligence: a sophisticated computer

deef: a person with a genetic defect

Eden: a secure area within the Urb where proovs live

Forbidden Zone, the: an area planted with land mines that separates Eden from the Urb

googan: an idiot

gummy: an old person

hide-or-cancel: a children's game

holoquarium: a holographic image of fish swimming in water

holoscape: a 3D illusion of a landcape

latch: a subdivision of the Urb controlled by a gang

latch-boss: a gang leader who controls territory in the Urb

looping: participating in a probe that repeats endlessly

luvmate: a lover

med-tek: a medical technician; like a doctor in the backtimes

microflash: a flashlight

mindprobe: a virtual reality experienced by your mind via an electrode needle

mope: dumb, lame (used as an adjective or a noun)

needlebrain: a person addicted to mindprobes

normal: a person who has not been genetically improved

Pipe, the: a tunnel system that used to transport water

proov: a genetically improved human

runner: a person who carries messages illegally between the latches

shooter: a violent mindprobe

splash, to: to kill

splat gun: a deadly weapon

stackbox: a concrete room used for storage in the backtimes, now used by squatters as homes

stunstik: a weapon that delivers an electric shock

takvee: a Tactical Urban Vehicle; an armored cyber-driven van

tek: a Technical Security Guard

trendie: a mindprobe about life in Eden

Urb, the: the area inhabited by normals

voicewriter: a machine that converts the spoken word into text

wheel: to drag a person in the street, tied to a jetbike

zoomed: crazy

The Next-to-Last Books in the Universe

Here are a few more books that look to the future and ask, "What if?":

Feed by M.T. Anderson
What if we had computer chips implanted in our brains — a constant feed of information, games, and advertising? Titus doesn't think about anything but what the feed tells him, until he meets Violet, a girl unlike anyone he's ever met.

Farenheit 451 by Ray Bradbury
In Spaz's world, people don't read books. In Guy Montag's world, they burn them. A classic novel about censorship and freedom.

The House of the Scorpion by Nancy Farmer
Matt is a clone — a genetic double of the most powerful man in Opium, El Patron. When El Patron dies, Matt begins a journey that will lead him to question everything he knows.

The Giver by Lois Lowry
Jonas lives in a structured community where there is no pain. But when he is chosen to become the community's Receiver of Memory, he must take on all the pain and suffering of the past.

1984 by George Orwell
Written in 1949, when 1984 *was* the future, this novel explores life in a society where the Thought Police can read your mind and where Big Brother is watching your every move.

The Last Book in the Universe
The Original Short Story

The Last Book in the Universe began as a short story for an anthology called *Tomorrowland: 10 Stories About the Future.* When Rodman Philbrick finished the story, he didn't want to stop writing because he knew Spaz had a lot more to say. Here are excerpts from the original short story.

If you're reading this, it must be a thousand years from now. Because nobody around here reads anymore. Why bother, when you can just probe it? Put all the images and excitement right inside your brain and let it rip. Trendies, shooters, sexbos — name it and you can probe it. Shooters are hot right now, but last year all anybody wanted to probe was a trendy.

Sexbos, they're *always* popular, even if nobody wants to admit it. Why that is, I can't say exactly, because I've never probed a sexbo or any of the other mindflicks. Not because I wouldn't like to, but because I've got this serious medical condition that means I'm allergic to electrode needle probes. Stick one of those in my brain and it'll kick off a really bad-seizure and then — total meltdown, lights out, that's all, folks.

Which really borks me. Because I'd love to probe a sexbo, if you want to know the truth. Just so I'd know what everybody else is talking about.

They call me Spaz, which is kind of a mope name, but I don't mind, not anymore. I'm talking into an old voicewriter program that prints out my words, because I was there when the Bully Bangers went to wheel the Ryter, and I saw what they saw, and I heard what they heard, and it kind of turned my brain around.

See, the Ryter was this old geez living in a little stackbox on the edge of the projos. A place where losers get stored, because they can't get anything better. Nobody owns the stackboxes, and if you squat in one long enough, I guess you can call it home — if home is a ten-by-ten concrete box stacked ten high, in rows of a hundred. Used to use 'em for prisons, before they came up with the mind fix for criminals.

There's no hydro in the stacks, no plumbing, no broadband, no nothing. Just the empty box and a door that looks like the lid on a sideways dumpster.

*   *   *

Anyhow, back to the old geez. The first thing that was different about him was he left his door open. See, I'm all jacked to kick the mutha down, but when I turn the corner the door is open, and my foot connects with nothing, just empty air. Which makes me feel like a real googan, and I guess he saw the look of it on my face.

"Could have happened to anybody," the geez says. He's kneeling on the floor by some old crate he'd fixed up as a desk, and he doesn't seem the least surprised about the bustdown. "Come on in," he goes, "make yourself at home."

I go, "Huh?" like, what are you, twisted? You *want* a bustdown? You *want* to get ripped? Are you mindsick or what? Except all I really say is "Huh?" because the rest is implied, which is a word I later got from the Ryter.

"I heard about the Bully Bangers giving me up," he says,

like it's no big deal. "Bound to happen sooner or later. Help yourself, son. Everything of value is over there in the corner."

He points out a gimme tote bag with a few crumball items inside. An old clock alarm vidscreen, a baseball mitt so old it isn't molded plastic, a coffee machine with the cord all neat and coiled. It doesn't amount to much, but there's enough for a few credits at the pawn mart. Better than usual for the stacks.

"Go on," he says. "Take it."

Normally I would, but there's something not normal about the whole situation. Like the way he coiled up the cord to the coffeemaker. You know you're going to get ripped, and you do that? Is it some kind of trick or what?

It's like he knows what I'm thinking, because the next thing he says is, "This isn't my first bustdown. Just thought I'd make it easier for us both."

"What else you got?" I say, closing in on the geez.

He smiles at me, which makes his old wrinkled face sort of glow, in a weird way. Like he wants an excuse to smile, no matter what happens. "What makes you think I've got anything else?" he asks, kind of craftylike.

That's when I see there are stacks of paper under the crate, and he's been sitting there in front of them, hoping I wouldn't notice. "What's this?" I go.

"Nothing of value," he says. "Just a book, if you want to know."

I scoff at him and snarl, "Liar! Books are in libraries. Or they used to be."

He starts to say something and then he stops, like I've given him something important to think about. "Hmmm," he goes. "You're aware that books used to be in libraries. That was before you were born, so how did you know?"

I shrug and go, "I heard is all. When I was a little kid. About how things used to be before the badtimes."

"And you remember everything you hear?"

"Pretty much," I say. "Doesn't everybody?"

The old geez chuckles. "Not hardly. Most of 'em, they've had their brains softened by probes and mindflicks, and they can't really retain much. Long-term memory is a thing of the past, no pun intended. The only ones left who can remember are a few old geezers like me. And, apparently, you."

Now that I think about it, I know what he's talking about. I've always had a lot of old stuff in my head that everybody else seems to have forgotten.

"What else do you remember?" the geez asks.

"What do you care?" I say.

The geez gives me a look, like he wants to memorize me or something. "That's what I do," he says. "I remember and I write it down. I take other people's memories, and I write those down, too. Of course, I change things to fit the story, but that's all part of the process."

"Process? You mean like a word processor?"

For some reason he finds that amusing. "Not exactly. Instead of using a computer to process the words, I do it directly. From my head to the page, writing down the words by hand, like they did in the backtimes. Of course, I used to use a voicewriter like everybody else, but it got ripped a couple of bustdowns ago. So now I do it this way," he says, showing me the stacks of paper covered with pen scratching. "Primitive, but it works."

"Yeah," I go. "You're doing it. But what are you doing?"

"Writing a book," he says. "The story of my life. The story of everybody's life, and the way things were when there used to be books."

"Nobody reads books anymore," I tell him.

He nods sadly. "I know. But someday that may change. And if and when it does, they'll want to know what happened, and why. They'll want stories that don't come out of a mind-probe needle. They'll want to read books again, someday."

"They?" I go. "Who do you mean?"

"Those who will be alive at some future date," he says.

Those who will be alive at some future date. I don't know why, but the way he says it gives me a shiver. Because I'd never thought about the future. You want to be down with the Bully Bangers, you can't think about the future. There's only room for the right here and the want-it-now. The future is like the moon. You never expect to go there or think about what it might be like. What's the point if you can't touch it or steal it?

"What's your story?" the geez asks, like he really wants to know.

I go, "I don't have a story."

Almost before I get the words out, he's shaking his head, like he knew what I was going to say and can't wait to disagree. "Everybody has a story," he says. "There are things about your life that are specific only to you. Secrets you know."

Finally the old geez is starting to make sense. And there's something about him I sort of like — or anyhow something I don't hate — so I sit there and listen to him jabber on about his book and all the stories and secrets he's been writing down for years, since before his hair went white and he got old.

*   *   *

Anyhow, what happened is I left without taking anything, and when I came back the next day it was like the Ryter was expecting me.

"I've been thinking about you, Spaz. About how you can still remember things. Every writer needs a reader. I figured my reader wasn't even born yet, but here you are."

I figure he must be making fun of me. "You think I care about those scratches you make on paper? Is that what you think?"

It's like there's an angry thing inside me that wants to bust out and hurt something, and right now what it wants to hurt is the old geezer, for laughing at me.

But his voice isn't laughing when he says, "I can teach you to read. That's not a problem. I'd like to teach you, if you'll let me. With a mind like yours — a mind that remembers — it won't take that long. A year or so, that's all. Maybe less."

That's when I go ahead and tell him the real secret, the one I didn't want to tell him yesterday. "You haven't got a year. The Bully Bangers are going to wheel you."

"You're sure about that?" he asks, looking worried. "I thought it was just another bustdown. I can handle getting ripped off, but I'll never survive getting dragged behind a jetbike."

Something makes me tell him, "You got to run away. Save yourself. Now, before it's too late."

The old geez sighs and looks at me with his soft eyes. "I'm too old to run. My running days are over." He thinks about something for a while, and I'm waiting because I know whatever it is, it's important. "I've got a better idea," he says. "You finish my book. Make it your own book."

*   *   *

He's starting to tell me about the old voicewriter programs when all of a sudden the Bully Bangers come for him. I hadn't expected them quite this soon, but here they are, swarming through the stacks like wild things. Shrieking and laughing and screaming all at the same time.

"Save my pages!" the old geez begs me as they come through the open door and grab him.

*   *   *

"Everybody has a story!" he chokes out as the rope gets tighter and the engines rev higher. "All you have to do is listen! You're my hope for the future, son! You're the only one left! You're the last book in the universe!"

The Bangers finally get bored and decide to end it. They gun their engines hard and drag the life out of him until there's nothing left. Nothing but silence, and the stink of jetbike fumes, and the bundle of rags and bones that used to be the Ryter.

I didn't stay until the very end. When the Ryter finally stopped telling his stories I ran away. I ran to the river, but there were dead things floating there, so I ran to the tallest building in the projos and climbed out on the roof and watched the sky, hoping maybe I'd see the shiny things called stars.

I never did.